For all enquiries regarding motion picture, television, and other media rights, please contact Samuel French.

MUSIC USE NOTE

Licensees are solely responsible for obtaining formal written permission from copyright owners to use copyrighted music in the performance of this play and are strongly cautioned to do so. If no such permission is obtained by the licensee, then the licensee must use only original music that the licensee owns and controls. Licensees are solely responsible and liable for all music clearances and shall indemnify the copyright owners of the play(s) and their licensing agent, Samuel French, against any costs, expenses, losses and liabilities arising from the use of music by licensees. Please contact the appropriate music licensing authority in your territory for the rights to any incidental music.

IMPORTANT BILLING AND CREDIT REQUIREMENTS

If you have obtained performance rights to this title, please refer to your licensing agreement for important billing and credit requirements.

D0207157

The cast of the THEATRE GUILD PRODUCTION as originally
presented at the GARRICK THEATRE, March 19th, 1923

THE ADDING MACHINE

A Play in Seven Scenes
By ELMER L. RICE

PRODUCTION DIRECTED BY PHILIP MOELLER
SETTINGS AND COSTUMES BY LEE SIMONSON
INCIDENTAL MUSIC BY DEEMS TAYLOR

CHARACTERS (IN ORDER OF APPEARANCE)

MR. ZERO...*Dudley Digges*
MRS. ZERO...*Helen Westley*
DAISY DIANA DOROTHEA DEVORE.............*Margaret Wycherly*
THE BOSS...*Irving Dillon*
MR. ONE...*Harry McKenna*
MRS. ONE...*Marcia Harris*
MR. TWO...*Paul Hayes*
MRS. TWO...*Theresa Stewart*
MR. THREE...*Gerald Lundegard*
MRS. THREE...*Georgiana Wilson*
MR. FOUR...*George Stehli*
MRS. FOUR...*Edith Burnett*
MR. FIVE...*William W. Griffith*
MRS. FIVE...*Ruby Craven*
MR. SIX...*Daniel Hamilton*
MRS. SIX...*Louise Sydmeth*
POLICEMAN...*Irving Dillon*
JUDY O'GRADY...*Elise Bartlett*
YOUNG MAN...*Gerald Lundegard*
SHRDLU...*Edward G. Robinson*
A HEAD...*Daniel Hamilton*
LIEUTENANT CHARLES.............................*Louis Calvert*
JOE...*William W. Griffith*

SCENE 1 A bedroom	SCENE 4 A place of justice	
SCENE 2 An office	SCENE 5 A graveyard	
SCENE 3 A living room	SCENE 6 A pleasant place	

Scene 7 Another office

STAGE MANAGER, LEWIS BARRINGTON

THE THEATRE GUILD, INC.

Board of Managers

Theresa Helburn   Philip Moeller   Lee Simonson
Lawrence Langner   Maurice Wertheim   Helen Westley

Executive Director: Theresa Helburn

Scenic Director	*Business Manager*	*Press Representative*
Lee Simonson	Warren P. Munsell	Ruth Benedict
Technical Director	*Play Reading Dept.*	*Stage Manager*
Carolyn Hancock	Courtenay Lemon	Robert L. Cook
	Ernest Boyd	

A FOREWORD

BY

PHILIP MOELLER

Before he wrote "The Adding Machine," Elmer Rice's name was associated with that type of theatrical production known as melodrama. Perhaps melodrama is best defined as the type of play in which the situation so to speak "creates" the people as over against that mightier form called tragedy in which the inevitable character of the dramatis personæ creates the situation. Undoubtedly it is much easier to work up a smashing idea for a scene and then invent the types that would fall into it than to breathe life into a list of characters that would have to evolve, because they are what they are, in the direction of this or that dénouement. Rice has worked assiduously and with great success at this type of play, and genuine praise is due to him. Though the average person doesn't suspect it, even the lesser thing when it comes to playwriting isn't easy. And to have written so great a hit in this genre as "On Trial" was something of an event in the American theatre. Probably no play of its type has had so great an acclaim as this, and it

A FOREWORD

was definitely interesting from the point of view of mere craftsmanship because aside from its merits as a thriller it was based on a scheme of dramatic technic which up to its time was probably unique, though since then the ever-recurrent "flash back" of the movies has made the trick an old story.

After "On Trial" Rice kept on writing this sort of play. Several others of this kind have been produced, and all of them with more or less success, but what must have been going on in his head all the time was something he probably but half realized, something which amounted to a desire in the creator's mind not only to do something else but to do something deeper. Perhaps the play of "the situation" was beginning to tire Mr. Rice a bit though not his public. Perhaps somewhere his subconscious mind was beginning to wonder just how tragedies evolved, perhaps the varied Muses that watch over the successful playwright were whispering in his ears and urging him to try something other, and these intimations of inspiration and his response thereto have resulted in "The Adding Machine," which to date is undoubtedly his most important work.

Now under what category of play does "The Adding Machine" belong? Recently there has crept into the mental vocabulary of people interested in the drama a term which originated in Germany and which is called "expressionism." The "expressionist" school is concerned with the difference between interpreting a character from the objective and the subjective point of view. Now if "expressionism" is objective seeing, as all observation must be, it is *subjective* projection; that is, all the half-understood "hinterland" thoughts, all the yearnings and unknown suppressions of the mind, are exposed, so to speak, in spite of the character, just as an X-ray exposes the inner structure of a thing as against its outer, more obvious and seeming form.

Thus expressionistically Mr. Rice has exposed the minds and souls of his people. Thus he has made their souls and shown us through their minds the way they use them. Pitilessly and pityingly, with a curious conglomeration of tenderness and scorn, he has studied the rich barrenness and the ridiculous unbeauty of these "white-collar" slaves. How many machine-forced minds are there who as the grind goes on and on are wishing to others these calamities of hate and for themselves these escapes in stumbling and half-articulate dreams. How many sex-starved Zeros are there who pilfer their poor gratification by peeping across the tenement airshafts, how many terrible parties are there such as Mr. Rice shows us which are going on night after night and in which people such as Mr. One and Mrs. Two and others like them are gathered "to give the air" to such baleful profundities. In short, how many souls are there who here, or hereafter, will be able to live up to a paradise—if there is one either here or hereafter—where everything will be of a bliss,

A FOREWORD

of a sort, that such souls can profit in and understand.

To my mind this is the real importance of Mr. Rice's play. I do not think that for a moment he means to imply that he believes necessarily in the philosophy of the hereafter which is expressed in his play, that his idea is that the Zero soul must of necessity go on and on through endless eternities to end in the endless sameness. This question of questionable immorality is secondary. What he has done and with withering insight is to expose the starved and bitter littleness and at the same time the huge universality of the Zero type, of the slave type, that from eternity to eternity expresses the futility and the tragedy of the mediocre spirit.

The Theatre Guild is proud to have produced Mr. Rice's play, and I cannot close this foreword without a word of thanks to him for his help through rehearsals, and for the splendid spirit of coöperation he has shown in our attempt to project "The Adding Machine," which to our minds ranks high among the contribution of the newer school of American drama, of that school already so rich in its accomplishment and so infinite in its possibilities.

CAST OF CHARACTERS

Mr. Zero
Mrs. Zero
Messrs. One, Two, Three, Four, Five, Six,
    and their respective wives
Daisy Diana Dorothea Devore
The Boss
Policeman
Two Attendants
Judy O'Grady
A Young Man
Shrdlu
A Head
Lieutenant Charles
Joe

ILLUSTRATIONS

THE ADDING MACHINE

SCENE ONE

[*SCENE: A bedroom.*

A small room containing an "installment plan" bed, dresser, and chairs. An ugly electric light fixture over the bed with a single glaring naked lamp. One small window with the shade drawn. The walls are papered with sheets of foolscap covered with columns of figures.

MR. ZERO is lying in the bed, facing the audience, his head and shoulders visible. He is thin, sallow, under-sized, and partially bald. MRS. ZERO is standing before the dresser arranging her hair for the night. She is forty-five, sharp-featured, gray streaks in her hair. She is shapeless in her long-sleeved cotton nightgown. She is wearing her shoes, over which sag her ungartered stockings.]

MRS. ZERO

[*As she takes down her hair*]: I'm gettin' sick o' them Westerns. All them cowboys ridin' around an' foolin' with them ropes. I don't care nothin' about that. I'm sick of 'em. I don't see why they don't

1

have more of them stories like "For Love's Sweet Sake."
I like them sweet little love stories. They're nice an'
wholesome. Mrs Twelve was sayin' to me only yesterday, "Mrs. Zero," says she, "what I like is one of them
wholesome stories, with just a sweet, simple little love
story." "You're right, Mrs. Twelve," I says. "That's
what I like, too." They're showin' too many Westerns
at the Rosebud. I'm gettin' sick of them. I think
we'll start goin' to the Peter Stuyvesant. They got
a good bill there Wednesday night. There's a Chubby
Delano comedy called "Sea-Sick." Mrs. Twelve was
tellin' me about it. She says it's a scream. They're
havin' a picnic in the country and they sit Chubby next
to an old maid with a great big mouth. So he gets
sore an' when she ain't lookin' he goes and catches a
frog and drops it in her clam chowder. An' when she
goes to eat the chowder the frog jumps out of it an'
right into her mouth. Talk about laugh! Mrs.
Twelve was tellin' me she laughed so she nearly passed
out. He sure can pull some funny ones. An' they
got that big Grace Darling feature, "A Mother's
Tears." She's sweet. But I don't like her clothes.
There's no style to them. Mrs. Nine was tellin' me she
read in *Pictureland* that she ain't livin' with her husband. He's her second, too. I don't know whether
they're divorced or just separated. You wouldn't
think it to see her on the screen. She looks so sweet
and innocent. Maybe it ain't true. You can't believe

all you read. They say some Pittsburgh millionaire
is crazy about her and that's why she ain't livin' with
her husband. Mrs. Seven was tellin' me her brother-
in-law has a friend that used to go to school with Grace
Darling. He says her name ain't Grace Darling at
all. Her right name is Elizabeth Dugan, he says, an'
all them stories about her gettin' five thousand a week
is the bunk, he says. She's sweet, though. Mrs. Eight
was tellin' me that "A Mother's Tears" is the best picture she ever made. "Don't miss it, Mrs. Zero," she
says. "It's sweet," she says. "Just sweet and wholesome. Cry!" she says, "I nearly cried my eyes out."
There's one part in it where this big bum of an Englishman—he's a married man, too—an' she's this little
simple country girl. An' she nearly falls for him, too.
But she's sittin' out in the garden, one day, and she
looks up and there's her mother lookin' at her, right
out of the clouds. So that night she locks the door
of her room. An' sure enough, when everybody's in
bed, along comes this big bum of an Englishman an'
when she won't let him in what does he do but go an'
kick open the door. "Don't miss it, Mrs. Zero," Mrs.
Eight was tellin' me. It's at the Peter Stuyvesant
Wednesday night, so don't be tellin' me you want to
go to the Rosebud. The Eights seen it downtown at
the Strand. They go downtown all the time. Just
like us—nit! I guess by the time it gets to the Peter
Stuyvesant all that part about kickin' in the door will

be cut out. Just like they cut out that big cabaret scene in "The Price of Virtue." They sure are pullin' some rough stuff in the pictures nowadays. "It's no place for a young girl," I was tellin' Mrs. Eleven, only the other day. An' by the time they get uptown half of it is cut out. But you wouldn't go downtown—not if wild horses was to drag you. You can wait till they come uptown! Well, I don't want to wait, see? I want to see 'em when everybody else is seein' them an' not a month later. Now don't go tellin' me you ain't got the price. You could dig up the price all right, all right, if you wanted to. I notice you always got the price to go to the ball game. But when it comes to me havin' a good time then it's always: "I ain't got the price, I gotta start savin'." A fat lot you'll ever save! I got all I can do now makin' both ends meet an' you talkin' about savin'. [*She seats herself on a chair and begins removing her shoes and stockings.*] An' don't go pullin' that stuff about bein' tired. "I been workin' hard all day. Twice a day in the subway's enough for me." Tired! Where do you get that tired stuff, anyhow? What about me? Where do I come in? Scrubbin' floors an' cookin' your meals an' washin' your dirty clothes. An' you sittin' on a chair all day, just addin' figgers an' waitin' for five-thirty. There's no five-thirty for me. I don't wait for no whistle. I don't get no vacations neither. And what's more I don't get no pay envelope every

Saturday night neither. I'd like to know where you'd be without me. An' what have I got to show for it?—slavin' my life away to give you a home. What's in it for me, I'd like to know? But it's my own fault, I guess. I was a fool for marryin' you. If I'd 'a' had any sense, I'd 'a' known what you were from the start. I wish I had it to do over again, I hope to tell you. You was goin' to do wonders, you was! You wasn't goin' to be a bookkeeper long—oh, no, not you. Wait till you got started—you was goin' to show 'em. There wasn't no job in the store that was too big for you. Well, I've been waitin'—waitin' for you to get started—see? It's been a good long wait, too. Twenty-five years! An' I ain't seen nothin' happen. Twenty-five years in the same job. Twenty-five years to-morrow! You're proud of it, ain't you? Twenty-five years in the same job an' never missed a day! That's somethin' to be proud of, ain't it? Sittin' for twenty-five years on the same chair, addin' up figures. What about bein' store-manager? I guess you forgot about that, didn't you? An' me at home here lookin' at the same four walls an' workin' my fingers to the bone to make both ends meet. Seven years since you got a raise! An' if you don't get one to-morrow, I'll bet a nickel you won't have the guts to go an' ask for one. I didn't pick much when I picked you, I'll tell the world. You ain't much to be proud of. [*She rises, goes to the window, and raises the shade. A few lighted win-*

dows are visible on the other side of the closed court. Looking out for a moment]: She ain't walkin' around to-night, you can bet your sweet life on that. An' she won't be walkin' around any more nights, neither. Not in this house, anyhow. [*She turns away from the window*]: The dirty bum! The idea of her comin' to live in a house with respectable people. They should 'a' gave her six years, not six months. If I was the judge I'd of gave her life. A bum like that. [*She approaches the bed and stands there a moment*]: I guess you're sorry she's gone. I guess you'd like to sit home every night an' watch her goin's-on. You're somethin' to be proud of, you are! [*She stands on the bed and turns out the light...A thin stream of moonlight filters in from the court. The two figures are dimly visible. MRS. ZERO gets into bed*]:

You'd better not start nothin' with women, if you know what's good for you. I've put up with a lot, but I won't put up with that. I've been slavin' away for twenty-five years, makin' a home for you an' nothin' to show for it. If you was any kind of a man you'd have a decent job by now an' I'd be gettin' some comfort out of life—instead of bein' just a slave, washin' pots an' standin' over the hot stove. I've stood it for twenty-five years an' I guess I'll have to stand it twenty-five more. But don't you go startin' nothin' with women—— [*She goes on talking as the curtain falls.*]

SCENE TWO

[*SCENE: An office in a department store. Wood and glass partitions. In the middle of the room, two tall desks back to back. At one desk on a high stool is* ZERO. *Opposite him at the other desk, also on a high stool, is* DAISY DIANA DOROTHEA DEVORE, *a plain, middle-aged woman. Both wear green eye shades and paper sleeve protectors. A pendent electric lamp throws light upon both desks.* DAISY *reads aloud figures from a pile of slips which lie before her. As she reads the figures,* ZERO *enters them upon a large square sheet of ruled paper which lies before him.*]

DAISY

[*Reading aloud*]: Three ninety-eight. Forty-two cents. A dollar fifty. A dollar fifty. A dollar twenty-five. Two dollars. Thirty-nine cents. Twenty-seven fifty.

ZERO

[*Petulantly*]: Speed it up a little, cancha?

DAISY

What's the rush? To-morrer's another day.

9

ZERO

Aw, you make me sick.

DAISY

An' you make me sicker.

ZERO

Go on. Go on. We're losin' time.

DAISY

Then quit bein' so bossy.

[*She reads*]: Three dollars. Two sixty-nine. Eighty-one fifty. Forty dollars. Eight seventy-five. Who do you think you are, anyhow?

ZERO

Never mind who I think I am. You tend to your work.

DAISY

Aw, don't be givin' me so many orders. Sixty cents. Twenty-four cents. Seventy-five cents. A dollar fifty. Two fifty. One fifty. One fifty. Two fifty. I don't have to take it from you and what's more I won't.

ZERO

Aw, quit talkin'.

DAISY

I'll talk all I want. Three dollars. Fifty cents. Fifty cents. Seven dollars. Fifty cents. Two fifty. Three fifty. Fifty cents. One fifty. Fifty cents.
[*She goes bending over the slips and transferring them from one pile to another. ZERO bends over his desk, busily entering the figures.*]

ZERO

[*Without looking up*]: You make me sick. Always shootin' off your face about somethin'. Talk, talk, talk. Just like all the other women. Women make me sick.

DAISY

[*Busily fingering the slips*]: Who do you think you are, anyhow? Bossin' me around. I don't have to take it from you, and what's more I won't.
[*They both attend closely to their work, neither looking up.*]

ZERO

Women make me sick. They're all alike. The judge gave her six months. I wonder what they do in the work-house. Peel potatoes. I'll bet she's sore at me. Maybe she'll try to kill me when she gets out. I better be careful. Hello, Girl Slays Betrayer.

Jealous Wife Slays Rival. You can't tell what a woman's liable to do. I better be careful.

DAISY

I'm gettin' sick of it. Always pickin' on me about somethin'. Never a decent word out of you. Not even the time o' day.

ZERO

I guess she wouldn't have the nerve at that. Maybe she don't even know it's me. They didn't even put my name in the paper, the big bums. Maybe she's been in the work-house before. A bum like that. She didn't have nothin' on that one time—nothin' but a shirt. [*He glances up quickly, then bends over again*]: You make me sick. I'm sick of lookin' at your face.

DAISY

Gee, ain't that whistle ever goin' to blow? You didn't used to be like that. Not even good mornin' or good evenin'. I ain't done nothin' to you. It's the young girls. Goin' around without corsets.

ZERO

Your face is gettin' all yeller. Why don't you put some paint on it? She was puttin' on paint that time. On her cheeks and on her lips. And that blue stuff on

her eyes. Just sittin' there in a shimmy puttin' on
the paint. An' walkin' around the room with her legs
all bare.

DAISY

I wish I was dead.

ZERO

I was a goddam fool to let the wife get on to me.
She oughta get six months at that. The dirty bum.
Livin' in a house with respectable people. She'd be
livin' there yet, if the wife hadn't o' got on to me.
Damn her!

DAISY

I wish I was dead.

ZERO

Maybe another one'll move in. Gee, that would be
great. But the wife's got her eye on me now.

DAISY

I'm scared to do it, though.

ZERO

You oughta move into that room. It's cheaper than
where you're livin' now. I better tell you about it.
I don't mean to be always pickin' on you.

DAISY

Gas. The smell of it makes me sick.
[ZERO *looks up and clears his throat.*]

DAISY

[*Looking up, startled*]: Whadja say?

ZERO

I didn't say nothin'.

DAISY

I thought you did.

ZERO

You thought wrong.
[*They bend over their work again.*]

DAISY

A dollar sixty. A dollar fifty. Two ninety. One sixty-two.

ZERO

Why the hell should I tell you? Fat chance of you forgettin' to pull down the shade!

DAISY

If I asked for carbolic they might get on to me.

ZERO

Your hair's gettin' gray. You don't wear them shirt waists any more with the low collars. When you'd bend down to pick somethin' up——

DAISY

I wish I knew what to ask for. Girl Takes Mercury After All-Night Party. Woman In Ten-Story Death Leap.

ZERO

I wonder where'll she go when she gets out. Gee, I'd like to make a date with her. Why didn't I go over there the night my wife went to Brooklyn? She never woulda found out.

DAISY

I seen Pauline Frederick do it once. Where could I get a pistol though?

ZERO

I guess I didn't have the nerve.

DAISY

I'll bet you'd be sorry then that you been so mean to me. How do I know, though? Maybe you wouldn't.

Zero

Nerve! I got as much nerve as anybody. I'm on the level, that's all. I'm a married man and I'm on the level.

Daisy

Anyhow, why ain't I got a right to live? I'm as good as anybody else. I'm too refined, I guess. That's the whole trouble.

Zero

The time the wife had pneumonia I thought she was goin' to pass out. But she didn't. The doctor's bill was eighty-seven dollars. [*Looking up*]: Hey, wait a minute! Didn't you say eighty-seven dollars?

Daisy

[*Looking up*]: What?

Zero

Was the last you said eighty-seven dollars?

Daisy

[*Consulting the slip*]: Forty-two fifty.

Zero

Well, I made a mistake. Wait a minute. [*He busies himself with an eraser*]: All right. Shoct

DAISY

Six dollars. Three fifteen. Two twenty-five. Sixty-five cents. A dollar twenty. You talk to me as if I was dirt.

ZERO

I wonder if I could kill the wife without anybody findin' out. In bed some night. With a pillow.

DAISY

I used to think you was stuck on me.

ZERO

I'd get found out, though. They always have ways.

DAISY

We used to be so nice and friendly together when I first came here. You used to talk to me then.

ZERO

Maybe she'll die soon. I noticed she was coughin' this mornin'.

DAISY

You used to tell me all kinds o' things. You were goin' to show them all. Just the same, you're still sittin' here.

ZERO

Then I could do what I damn please. Oh, boy!

DAISY

Maybe it ain't all your fault neither. Maybe if you'd had the right kind o' wife—somebody with a lot of common-sense, somebody refined—me!

ZERO

At that, I guess I'd get tired of bummin' around. A feller wants some place to hang his hat.

DAISY

I wish she would die.

ZERO

And when you start goin' with women you're liable to get into trouble. And lose your job maybe.

DAISY

Maybe you'd marry me.

ZERO

Gee, I wish I'd gone over there that night.

DAISY

Then I could quit workin'.

Zero

Lots o' women would be glad to get me.

Daisy

You could look a long time before you'd find a sensible, refined girl like me.

Zero

Yes, sir, they could look a long time before they'd find a steady meal-ticket like me.

Daisy

I guess I'd be too old to have any kids. They say it ain't safe after thirty-five.

Zero

Maybe I'd marry you. You might be all right, at that.

Daisy

I wonder—if you don't want kids—whether—if there's any way——

Zero

[*Looking up*]: Hey! Hey! Can't you slow up? What do you think I am—a machine?

DAISY

[*Looking up*]: Say, what do you want, anyhow? First it's too slow an' then it's too fast. I guess you don't know what you want.

ZERO

Well, never mind about that. Just you slow up.

DAISY

I'm gettin' sick o' this. I'm goin' to ask to be transferred.

ZERO

Go ahead. You can't make me mad.

DAISY

Aw, keep quiet. [*She reads*]: Two forty-five. A dollar twenty. A dollar fifty. Ninety cents. Sixty-three cents.

ZERO

Marry you! I guess not! You'd be as bad as the one I got.

DAISY

You wouldn't care if I did ask. I got a good mind to ask.

ZERO

I was a fool to get married.

DAISY

Then I'd never see you at all.

ZERO

What chance has a guy got with a woman tied around his neck?

DAISY

That time at the store picnic—the year your wife couldn't come—you were nice to me then.

ZERO

Twenty-five years holdin' down the same job!

DAISY

We were together all day—just sittin' around under the trees.

ZERO

I wonder if the boss remembers about it bein' twenty-five years.

DAISY

And comin' home that night—you sat next to me in the big delivery wagon.

ZERO

I got a hunch there's a big raise comin' to me.

DAISY

I wonder what it feels like to be really kissed.   Men
—dirty pigs!   They want the bold ones.

ZERO

If he don't come across I'm goin' right up to the
front office and tell him where he gets off.

DAISY

I wish I was dead.

ZERO

"Boss," I'll say, "I want to have a talk with you."
"Sure," he'll say, "sit down.   Have a Corona Corona."
"No," I'll say, "I don't smoke."   "How's that?" he'll
say.   "Well, boss," I'll say, "it's this way.   Every
time I feel like smokin' I just take a nickel and put it
in the old sock.   A penny saved is a penny earned,
that's the way I look at it."   "Damn sensible," he'll
say.   "You got a wise head on you, Zero."

DAISY

I can't stand the smell of gas.   It makes me sick.
You coulda kissed me if you wanted to.

Zero

"Boss," I'll say, "I ain't quite satisfied. I been on the job twenty-five years now and if I'm gonna stay I gotta see a future ahead of me." "Zero," he'll say, "I'm glad you came in. I've had my eye on you, Zero. Nothin' gets by me." "Oh, I know that, boss," I'll say. That'll hand him a good laugh, that will. "You're a valuable man, Zero," he'll say, "and I want you right up here with me in the front office. You're done addin' figgers. Monday mornin' you move up here."

Daisy

Them kisses in the movies—them long ones—right on the mouth——

Zero

I'll keep a-goin' right on up after that. I'll show some of them birds where they get off.

Daisy

That one the other night—"The Devil's Alibi"—he put his arms around her—and her head fell back and her eyes closed—like she was in a daze.

Zero

Just give me about two years and I'll show them birds where they get off.

Daisy

I guess that's what it's like—a kinda daze—when I see them like that, I just seem to forget everything.

Zero

Then me for a place in Jersey.   And maybe a little Buick.   No tin Lizzie for mine.   Wait till I get started—I'll show 'em.

Daisy

I can see it now when I kinda half-close my eyes. The way her head fell back.   And his mouth pressed right up against hers.   Oh, Gawd! it must be grand! [*There is a sudden shrill blast from a steam whistle.*]

Daisy and Zero

[*Together*]:   The whistle!
[*With great agility they get off their stools, remove their eye shades and sleeve protectors and put them on the desks. Then each produces from behind the desk a hat—*Zero, *a dusty derby,* Daisy, *a frowsy straw...* Daisy *puts on her hat and turns toward* Zero *as though she were about to speak to him. But he is busy cleaning his pen and pays no attention to her. She sighs and goes toward the door at the left.*]

Zero

[*Looking up*]: G'night, Miss Devore.
[*But she does not hear him and exits. Zero takes up
    his hat and goes left. The door at the right opens
    and the* Boss *enters—middle-aged, stoutish, bald,
    well-dressed.*]

The Boss

[*Calling*]: Oh—er—Mister—er——
[Zero *turns in surprise, sees who it is and trembles
    nervously.*]

Zero

[*Obsequiously*]: Yes, sir. Do you want me, sir?

Boss

Yes. Just come here a moment, will you?

Zero

Yes, sir. Right away, sir. [*He fumbles his hat, picks
it up, stumbles, recovers himself, and approaches the
Boss, every fibre quivering.*]

Boss

Mister—er—er——

Zero

Zero.

Boss

Yes, Mr. Zero.   I wanted to have a little talk with you.

Zero

[*With a nervous grin*]:   Yes sir, I been kinda expectin' it.

Boss

[*Staring at him*]:   Oh, have you?

Zero

Yes, sir.

Boss

How long have you been with us, Mister--er—Mister——

Zero

Zero.

Boss

Yes, Mister Zero.

Zero

Twenty-five years to-day.

Boss

Twenty-five years!   That's a long time.

Zero

Never missed a day.

Boss

And you've been doing the same work all the time?

Zero

Yes, sir.   Right here at this desk.

Boss

Then, in that case, a change probably won't be un-welcome to you.

Zero

No, sir, it won't.   And that's the truth.

Boss

We've been planning a change in this department for some time.

Zero

I kinda thought you had your eye on me.

Boss

You were right. The fact is that my efficiency experts have recommended the installation of adding machines.

Zero

[*Staring at him*]: Addin' machines?

Boss

Yes, you've probably seen them. A mechanical device that adds automatically.

Zero

Sure. I've seen them. Keys—and a handle that you pull. [*He goes through the motions in the air.*]

Boss

That's it. They do the work in half the time and a high-school girl can operate them. Now, of course, I'm sorry to lose an old and faithful employee——

Zero

Excuse me, but would you mind sayin' that again?

Boss

I say I'm sorry to lose an employee who's been with me for so many years——

[*Soft music is heard—the sound of the mechanical player of a distant merry-go-round.   The part of the floor upon which the desk and stools are standing begins to revolve very slowly.*]

Boss

But, of course, in an organization like this, efficiency must be the first consideration——
[*The music becomes gradually louder and the revolutions more rapid.*]

Boss

You will draw your salary for the full month.   And I'll direct my secretary to give you a letter of recommendation——

Zero

Wait a minute, boss.   Let me get this right.   You mean I'm canned?

Boss

[*Barely making himself heard above the increasing volume of sound*]:   I'm sorry—no other alternative—greatly regret—old employee—efficiency—economy—business—*business*—BUSINESS——
[*His voice is drowned by the music.   The platform is revolving rapidly now.   Zero and the Boss face each other.   They are entirely motionless save*

for the Boss's *jaws, which open and close inces-
santly. But the words are inaudible. The music
swells and swells. To it is added every off-stage
effect of the theatre: the wind, the waves, the gal-
loping horses, the locomotive whistle, the sleigh
bells, the automobile siren, the glass-crash. New
Year's Eve, Election Night, Armistice Day, and
the Mardi-Gras. The noise is deafening, maddening, unendurable. Suddenly it culminates in a
terrific peal of thunder. For an instant there is
a flash of red and then everything is plunged into
blackness.*]

[*Curtain*]

SCENE THREE

[SCENE: The ZERO dining room. Entrance door at right. Doors to kitchen and bedroom at left. The walls, as in the first scene, are papered with foolscap sheets covered with columns of figures. In the middle of the room, upstage, a table set for two. Along each side wall, seven chairs are ranged in symmetrical rows.

At the rise of the curtain MRS. ZERO is seen seated at the table looking alternately at the entrance door and a clock on the wall. She wears a bungalow apron over her best dress.

After a few moments, the entrance door opens and ZERO enters. He hangs his hat on a rack behind the door and coming over to the table seats himself at the vacant place. His movements throughout are quiet and abstracted.]

MRS. ZERO

[Breaking the silence]: Well, it was nice of you to come home. You're only an hour late and that ain't very much. The supper don't get very cold in an hour. An' of course the part about our havin' a lot of company to-night don't matter.
[They begin to eat.]

Ain't you even got sense enough to come home on time? Didn't I tell you we're goin' to have a lot o' company to-night? Didn't you know the Ones are comin'? An' the Twos? An' the Threes? An' the Fours? An' the Fives? And the Sixes? Didn't I tell you to be home on time? I might as well talk to a stone wall.

[*They eat for a few moments in silence.*]

I guess you musta had some important business to attend to. Like watchin' the score-board. Or was two kids havin' a fight an' you was the referee? You sure do have a lot of business to attend to. It's a wonder you have time to come home at all. You gotta tough life, you have. Walk in, hang up your hat, an' put on the nose-bag. An' me in the hot kitchen all day, cookin' your supper an' waitin' for you to get good an' ready to come home!

[*Again they eat in silence.*]

Maybe the boss kept you late to-night. Tellin' you what a big noise you are and how the store couldn't 'a' got along if you hadn't been pushin' a pen for twenty-five years. Where's the gold medal he pinned on you? Did some blind old lady take it away from you or did you leave it on the seat of the boss's limousine when he brought you home?

[*Again a few moments of silence.*]

I'll bet he gave you a big raise, didn't he? Promoted you from the third floor to the fourth, maybe.

Raise? A fat chance you got o' gettin' a raise. All they gotta do is put an ad in the paper. There's ten thousand like you layin' around the streets. You'll be holdin' down the same job at the end of another twenty-five years—if you ain't forgot how to add by that time.

[*A noise is heard off-stage, a sharp clicking such as is made by the operation of the keys and levers of an adding machine. ZERO raises his head for a moment, but lowers it almost instantly.*]

MRS. ZERO

There's the door-bell. The company's here already. And we ain't hardly finished supper.

[*She rises.*]

But I'm goin' to clear off the table whether you're finished or not. If you want your supper, you got a right to be home on time. Not standin' around lookin' at score-boards.

[*As she piles up the dishes, ZERO rises and goes toward the entrance door.*]

Wait a minute! Don't open the door yet. Do you want the company to see all the mess? An' go an' put on a clean collar. You got red ink all over it.

[*ZERO goes toward bedroom door.*]

I should think after pushin' a pen for twenty-five years, you'd learn how to do it without gettin' ink on your collar.

[ZERO *exits to bedroom. MRS. ZERO takes dishes to kitchen talking as she goes.*]

I guess I can stay up all night now washin' dishes. You should worry! That's what a man's got a wife for, ain't it? Don't he buy her her clothes an' let her eat with him at the same table? An' all she's gotta do is cook the meals an' do the washin' an' scrub the floor, an' wash the dishes, when the company goes. But, believe me, you're goin' to sling a mean dish-towel when the company goes to-night!

[*While she is talking ZERO enters from bedroom. He wears a clean collar and is cramming the soiled one furtively into his pocket. MRS. ZERO enters from kitchen. She has removed her apron and carries a table cover which she spreads hastily over the table. The clicking noise is heard again.*]

MRS. ZERO

There's the bell again. Open the door, cancha?

ZERO *goes to the entrance door and opens it. Six men and six women file into the room in a double column. The men are all shapes and sizes, but their dress is identical with that of Zero in every detail. Each, however, wears a wig of a different color. The women are all dressed alike, too, except that the dress of each is of a different color.*]

Mrs. Zero

[*Taking the first woman's hand*]:   How de do, Mrs. One.

Mrs. One

How de do, Mrs. Zero.

[Mrs. Zero *repeats this formula with each woman in turn. Zero does the same with the men except that he is silent throughout. The files now separate, each man taking a chair from the right wall and each woman one from the left wall. Each sex forms a circle with the chairs very close together. The men—all except Zero—smoke cigars. The women munch chocolates.*]

Six

Some rain we're havin'.

Five

Never saw the like of it.

Four

Worst in fourteen years, paper says.

Three

Y'can't always go by the papers.

Two

No, that's right, too.

One

We're liable to forget from year to year.

Six

Yeh, come t' think, last year was pretty bad, too.

Five

An' how about two years ago?

Four

Still this year's pretty bad.

Three

Yeh, no gettin' away from that.

Two

Might be a whole lot worse.

One

Yeh, it's all the way you look at it.   Some rain, though.

Mrs. Six

I like them little organdie dresses.

MRS. FIVE

Yeh, with a little lace trimmin' on the sleeves.

MRS. FOUR

Well, I like 'em plain myself.

MRS. THREE

Yeh, what I always say is the plainer the more refined.

MRS. TWO

Well, I don't think a little lace does any harm.

MRS. ONE

No, it kinda dresses it up.

MRS. ZERO

Well, I always say it's all a matter of taste.

MRS. SIX

I saw you at the Rosebud Movie Thursday night, Mr. One.

ONE

Pretty punk show, I'll say.

Two

They're gettin' worse all the time.

Mrs. Six

But who was the charming lady, Mr. One?

One

Now don't you go makin' trouble for me. That was my sister.

Mrs. Five

Oho! That's what they all say.

Mrs. Four

Never mind! I'll bet Mrs. One knows what's what, all right.

Mrs. One

Oh, well, he can do what he likes—'slong as he behaves himself.

Three

You're in luck at that, One. Fat chance I got of gettin' away from the frau even with my sister.

Mrs. Three

You oughta be glad you got a good wife to look after you.

THE OTHER WOMEN

[*In unison*]: That's right, Mrs. Three.

FIVE

I guess I know who wears the pants in your house, Three.

MRS. ZERO

Never mind. I saw them holdin' hands at the movie the other night.

THREE

She musta been tryin' to get some money away from me.

MRS. THREE

Swell chance anybody'd have of gettin' any money away from you.

[*General laughter.*]

FOUR

They sure are a loving couple.

MRS. TWO

Well, I think we oughta change the subject.

MRS. ONE

Yes, let's change the subject.

Six

[*Sotto voce*]: Did you hear the one about the travellin' salesman?

Five

It seems this guy was in a sleeper.

Four

Goin' from Albany to San Diego.

Three

And in the next berth was an old maid.

Two

With a wooden leg.

One

Well, along about midnight——
[*They all put their heads together and whisper.*]

Mrs. Six

[*Sotto voce*]: Did you hear about the Sevens?

Mrs. Five

They're gettin' a divorce.

Mrs. Four

It's the second time for him.

Mrs. Three

They're two of a kind, if you ask me.

Mrs. Two

One's as bad as the other.

Mrs. One

Worse.

Mrs. Zero

They say that she——
[*They all put their heads together and whisper.*]

Six

I think this woman suffrage is the bunk.

Five

It sure is!   Politics is a man's business.

Four

Woman's place is in the home.

Three

That's it! Lookin' after the kids, 'stead of hangin' around the streets.

Two

You hit the nail on the head that time.

One

The trouble is they don't know what they want.

Mrs. Six

Men sure get me tired.

Mrs. Five

They sure are a lazy lot.

Mrs. Four

And dirty.

Mrs. Three

Always grumblin' about somethin'.

Mrs. Two

When they're not lyin'!

Mrs. One

Or messin' up the house.

Mrs. Zero

Well, believe me, I tell mine where he gets off.

Six

Business conditions are sure bad.

Five

Never been worse.

Four

I don't know what we're comin' to.

Three

I look for a big smash-up in about three months.

Two

Wouldn't surprise me a bit.

One

We're sure headin' for trouble.

Mrs. Six

My aunt has gall-stones.

Mrs. Five

My husband has bunions.

MRS. FOUR

My sister expects next month.

MRS. THREE

My cousin's husband has erysipelas.

MRS. TWO

My niece has St. Vitus's dance.

MRS. ONE

My boy has fits.

MRS. ZERO

I never felt better in my life. Knock wood!

SIX

Too damn much agitation, that's at the bottom of it.

FIVE

That's it! too damn many strikes.

FOUR

Foreign agitators, that's what it is.

THREE

They ought be run outa the country.

Two

What the hell do they want, anyhow?

One

They don't know what they want, if you ask me.

Six

America for the Americans is what I say!

All

[*In unison*]: That's it! Damn foreigners! Damn dagoes! Damn Catholics! Damn sheenies! Damn niggers! Jail 'em! shoot 'em! hang 'em! lynch 'em! burn 'em!

[*They all rise.*]

All

[*Sing in unison*]: "My country' tis of thee,
Sweet land of liberty!"

Mrs. Four

Why so pensive, Mr. Zero?

Zero

[*Speaking for the first time*]: I'm thinkin'.

Mrs. Four

Well, be careful not to sprain your mind.
[*Laughter.*]

Mrs. Zero

Look at the poor men all by themselves.   We ain't
very sociable.

One

Looks like we're neglectin' the ladies.
[*The women cross the room and join the men, all chat-
     tering loudly.   The door-bell rings.*]

Mrs. Zero

Sh!   The door-bell!
[*The volume of sound slowly diminishes.   Again the
     door-bell.*]

Zero

[*Quietly*]:   I'll go.   It's for me.
[*They watch curiously as* Zero *goes to the door and
     opens it, admitting a policeman.   There is a mur-
     mur of surprise and excitement.*]

Policeman

I'm lookin' for Mr. Zero.
[*They all point to* Zero.]

ZERO

I've been expectin' you.

POLICEMAN

Come along!

ZERO

Just a minute. [*He puts his hand in his pocket.*]

POLICEMAN

What's he tryin' to pull? [*He draws a revolver.*] I got you covered.

ZERO

Sure, that's all right. I just want to give you somethin'. [*He takes the collar from his pocket and gives it to the policeman.*]

POLICEMAN

[*Suspiciously*]: What's that?

ZERO

The collar I wore.

POLICEMAN

What do I want it for?

ZERO

It's got blood-stains on it.

POLICEMAN

[*Pocketing it*]: All right, come along!

ZERO

[*Turning to* MRS. ZERO]: I gotta go with him. You'll have to dry the dishes yourself.

MRS. ZERO

[*Rushing forward*]: What are they takin' you for?

ZERO

[*Calmly*]: I killed the boss this afternoon.
[*Quick Curtain as the policeman takes him off*.]

SCENE FOUR

[*SCENE: A court of justice. Three bare white walls without door or windows except for a single door in the right wall. At the right is a jury-box in which are seated* MESSRS. ONE, TWO, THREE, FOUR, FIVE, *and* SIX *and their respective wives. On either side of the jury box stands a uniformed* OFFICER. *Opposite the jury box is a long, bare oak table piled high with law books. Behind the books* ZERO *is seated, his face buried in his hands. There is no other furniture in the room. A moment after the rise of the curtain, one of the officers rises and going around the table, taps* ZERO *on the shoulder.* ZERO *rises and accompanies the officer. The* OFFICER *escorts him to the great empty space in the middle of the court room, facing the jury. He motions to* ZERO *to stop, then points to the jury and resumes his place beside the jury-box.* ZERO *stands there looking at the jury, bewildered and half afraid. The* JURORS *give no sign of having seen him. Throughout they sit with folded arms, staring stolidly before them.*]

ZERO

[*Beginning to speak; haltingly*]: Sure I killed him. I ain't sayin' I didn't, am I? Sure I killed him. Them

lawyers! They give me a good stiff pain, that's what
they give me. Half the time I don't know what the
hell they're talkin' about. Objection sustained. Objection over-ruled. What's the big idea, anyhow? You
ain't heard me do any objectin', have you? Sure not!
What's the idea of objectin'? You got a right to
know. What I say is if one bird kills another bird,
why you got a right to call him for it. That's what I
say. I know all about that. I been on the jury, too.
Them lawyers! Don't let 'em fill you full of bunk.
All that bull about it bein' red ink on the bill-file. Red
ink nothin'! It was blood, see? I want you to get
that right. I killed him, see? Right through the
heart with the bill-file, see? I want you to get that
right—all of you. One, two, three, four, five, six, seven,
eight, nine, ten, eleven, twelve. Twelve of you. Six
and six. That makes twelve. I figgered it up often
enough. Six and six makes twelve. And five is seven-
teen. And eight is twenty-five. And three is twenty-
eight. Eight and carry two. Aw, cut it out! Them
damn figgers! I can't forget 'em. Twenty-five
years, see? Eight hours a day, exceptin' Sundays.
And July and August half-day Saturday. One week's
vacation with pay. And another week without pay if
you want it. Who the hell wants it? Layin' around
the house listenin' to the wife tellin' you where you get
off. Nix! An' legal holidays. I nearly forgot them.
New Year's, Washington's Birthday, Decoration Day,

Fourth o' July, Labor Day, Election Day, Thanks-givin', Christmas. Good Friday if you want it. An' if you're a Jew, Young Kipper an' the other one—I for-get what they call it. The dirty sheenies—always gettin' two to the other bird's one. An' when a holi-day comes on Sunday, you get Monday off. So that's fair enough. But when the Fourth o' July comes on Saturday, why you're out o' luck on account of Sat-urday bein' a half-day anyhow. Get me? Twenty-five years—I'll tell you somethin' funny. Decoration Day an' the Fourth o' July are always on the same day o' the week. Twenty-five years. Never missed a day, and never more'n five minutes late. Look at my time card if you don't believe me. Eight twenty-seven, eight thirty, eight twenty-nine, eight twenty-seven, eight thirty-two. Eight an' thirty-two's forty an'—— Goddam them figgers! I can't forget 'em. They're funny things, them figgers. They look like people sometimes. The eights, see? Two dots for the eyes and a dot for the nose. An' a line. That's the mouth, see? An' there's others remind you of other things— but I can't talk about them, on account of there bein' ladies here. Sure I killed him. Why didn't he shut up? If he'd only shut up! Instead o' talkin' an' talkin' about how sorry he was an' what a good guy I was an' this an' that. I felt like sayin' to him: "For Christ's sake, shut up!" But I didn't have the nerve, see? I didn't have the nerve to say that to the boss.

An' he went on talkin', sayin' how sorry he was, see?
He was standin' right close to me. An' his coat only
had two buttons on it. Two an' two makes four an'—
aw, can it! An' there was the bill-file on the desk.
Right where I could touch it. It ain't right to kill a
guy. I know that. When I read all about him in the
paper an' about his three kids I felt like a cheap skate,
I tell you. They had the kids' pictures in the paper,
right next to mine. An' his wife, too. Gee, it must
be swell to have a wife like that. Some guys sure is
lucky. An' he left fifty thousand dollars just for a
rest-room for the girls in the store. He was a good
guy, at that. Fifty thousand. That's more'n twice
as much as I'd have if I saved every nickel I ever made.
Let's see. Twenty-five an' twenty-five an' twenty-five
an'—aw, cut it out! An' the ads had a big, black
border around 'em; an' all it said was that the store
would be closed for three days on account of the boss
bein' dead. That nearly handed me a laugh, that did.
All them floor-walkers an' buyers an' high-muck-a-
mucks havin' me to thank for gettin' three days off. I
hadn't oughta killed him. I ain't sayin' nothin' about
that. But I thought he was goin' to give me a raise,
see? On account of bein' there twenty-five years. He
never talked to me before, see? Except one mornin'
we happened to come in the store together and I held
the door open for him and he said "Thanks." Just
like that, see? "Thanks!" That was the only time

he ever talked to me. An' when I seen him comin' up to my desk, I didn't know where I got off. A big guy like that comin' up to my desk. I felt like I was chokin' like and all of a sudden I got a kind o' bad taste in my mouth like when you get up in the mornin'. I didn't have no right to kill him. The district attorney is right about that. He read the law to you, right out o' the book. Killin' a bird—that's wrong. But there was that girl, see? Six months they gave her. It was a dirty trick tellin' the cops on her like that. I shouldn't 'a' done that. But what was I gonna do? The wife wouldn't let up on me. I hadda do it. She used to walk around the room, just in her undershirt, see? Nothin' else on. Just her undershirt. An' they gave her six months. That's the last I'll ever see of her. Them birds—how do they get away with it? Just grabbin' women, the way you see 'em do in the pictures. I've seen lots I'd like to grab like that, but I ain't got the nerve—in the subway an' on the street an' in the store buyin' things. Pretty soft for them shoe-salesmen, I'll say, lookin' at women's legs all day. Them lawyers! They give me a pain, I tell you—a pain! Sayin' the same thing over an' over again. I never said I didn't kill him. But that ain't the same as bein' a regular murderer. What good did it do me to kill him? I didn't make nothin' out of it. Answer yes or no! Yes or no, me elbow! There's some things you can't answer yes or no. Give me the once-over, you

guys. Do I look like a murderer? Do I? I never
did no harm to nobody. Ask the wife. She'll tell
you. Ask anybody. I never got into trouble. You
wouldn't count that one time at the Polo Grounds.
That was just fun like. Everybody was yellin', "Kill
the empire! Kill the empire!" An' before I knew
what I was doin' I fired the pop bottle. It was on account of everybody yellin' like that. Just in fun like,
see? The yeller dog! Callin' that one a strike—a
mile away from the plate. Anyhow, the bottle didn't
hit him. An' when I seen the cop comin' up the aisle,
I beat it. That didn't hurt nobody. It was just in
fun like, see? An' that time in the subway. I was
readin' about a lynchin', see? Down in Georgia.
They took the nigger an' they tied him to a tree.
An' they poured kerosene on him and lit a big fire
under him. The dirty nigger! Boy, I'd of liked to
been there, with a gat in each hand, pumpin' him full
of lead. I was readin' about it in the subway, see?
Right at Times Square where the big crowd gets on.
An' all of a sudden this big nigger steps right on my
foot. It was lucky for him I didn't have a gun on
me. I'd of killed him sure, I guess. I guess he
couldn't help it all right on account of the crowd, but
a nigger's got no right to step on a white man's foot.
I told him where he got off all right. The dirty nigger.
But that didn't hurt nobody, either. I'm a pretty
steady guy, you gotta admit that. Twenty-five years

in one job an' I never missed a day.   Fifty-two weeks
in a year. Fifty-two an' fifty-two an' fifty-two an'——
They didn't have t' look for me, did they?   I didn't
try to run away, did I?   Where was I goin' to run to!
I wasn't thinkin' about it at all, see?   I'll tell you
what I was thinkin' about—how I was goin' to break
it to the wife about bein' canned.   He canned me after
twenty-five years, see?   Did the lawyers tell you about
that?   I forget.   All that talk gives me a headache.
Objection sustained.   Objection over-ruled.   Answer
yes or no.   It gives me a headache.   And I can't get
the figgers outta my head, neither.   But that's what
I was thinkin' about—how I was goin' t' break it to
the wife about bein' canned.   An' what Miss Devore
would think when she heard about me killin' him.   I
bet she never thought I had the nerve to do it.   I'd
of married her if the wife had passed out.   I'd be
holdin' down my job yet, if he hadn't o' canned me.
But he kept talkin' an' talkin'.   An' there was the bill-
file right where I could reach it.   Do you get me?
I'm just a regular guy like anybody else.   Like you
birds, now.

[*For the first time the* JURORS *relax, looking indig-
nantly at each other and whispering.*]

Suppose you was me, now.   Maybe you'd 'a' done the
same thing.   That's the way you oughta look at it,
see?   Suppose you was me——

The Jurors

[*Rising as one and shouting in unison*]: *GUILTY!*
[Zero *falls back, stunned for a moment by their vocif-
erousness. The* Jurors *right-face in their places
and file quickly out of the jury-box and toward
the door in a double column.*]

Zero

[*Recovering speech as the* Jurors *pass out at the
door*]: Wait a minute. Jest a minute. You don't
get me right. Jest give me a chance an' I'll tell you
how it was. I'm all mixed up, see? On account of
them lawyers. And the figgers in my head. But I'm
goin' to tell you how it was. I was there twenty-five
years, see? An' they gave her six months, see?
[*He goes on haranguing the empty jury-box as the
curtain falls.*]

SCENE FIVE

[*SCENE: A grave-yard in full moonlight. It is a second-rate grave-yard—no elaborate tombstones or monuments—just simple headstones and here and there a cross. At the back is an iron fence with a gate in the middle. At first no one is visible, but there are occasional sounds throughout: the hooting of an owl, the whistle of a distant whippoorwill, the croaking of a bull-frog, and the yowling of a serenading cat. After a few moments two figures appear outside the gate— a man and a woman. She pushes the gate and it opens with a rusty creak. The couple enter. They are now fully visible in the moonlight—*JUDY O'GRADY *and a* YOUNG MAN.]

JUDY

[*Advancing*]: Come on, this is the place.

YOUNG MAN

[*Hanging back*]: This! Why this here is a cemetery.

JUDY

Aw, quit yer kiddin'!

YOUNG MAN

You don't mean to say——

JUDY

What's the matter with this place?

YOUNG MAN

A cemetery!

JUDY

Sure. What of it?

YOUNG MAN

You must be crazy.

JUDY

This place is all right, I tell you. I been here lots o' times.

YOUNG MAN

Nix on this place for me!

JUDY

Ain't this place as good as another? Whaddya afraid of? They're all dead ones here! They don't bother you.

[*With sudden interest*]: Oh, look, here's a new one.

YOUNG MAN

Come on out of here.

JUDY

Wait a minute. Let's see what it says. [*She kneels on a grave in the foreground and putting her face close to headstone spells out the inscription*]: Z-E-R-O. Z-e-r-o. Zero! Say, that's the guy——

YOUNG MAN

Zero? He's the guy killed his boss, ain't he?

JUDY

Yeh, that's him, all right. But what I'm thinkin' of is that I went to the hoose-gow on account of him.

YOUNG MAN

What for?

JUDY

You know, same old stuff. Tenement House Law. [*Mincingly*]: Section blaa-blaa of the Penal Code. Third offense. Six months.

YOUNG MAN

And this bird——

JUDY

[*Contemptuously*]: Him? He was mama's white-haired boy. We lived in the same house. Across the airshaft, see? I used to see him lookin' in my window. I guess his wife musta seen him, too. Anyhow, they went and turned the bulls on me. And now I'm out and he's in. [*Suddenly*]: Say—say—— [*She bursts into a peal of laughter.*]

YOUNG MAN

[*Nervously*]: What's so funny?

JUDY

[*Rocking with laughter*]: Say, wouldn't it be funny —if—if—— [*She explodes again*]: That would be a good joke on him, all right. He can't do nothin' about it now, can he?

YOUNG MAN

Come on out of here. I don't like this place.

JUDY

Aw, you're a bum sport. What do you want to spoil my joke for?
[*A cat yammers mellifluously.*]

SHRDLU

lps keep the mosquitoes away. [He lights

SHRDLU

taking the cigarette out of his mouth]:
if I smoke, Mr.—Mr.——?

ZERO

ht ahead.

SHRDLU

g the cigarette]: Thank you. I didn't
name.
not reply.]

SHRDLU

I say I didn't catch your name.

ZERO

you the first time. [Hesitantly]: I'm
ell you who I am and what I done, you'll be

SHRDLU

No matter what your sins may be, they
compared to mine.

YOUNG MAN

[Half hysterically]: What's that?

JUDY

It's only the cats. They seem to like it here all
right. But come on if you're afraid. [They go
toward the gate. As they go out]: You nervous men
sure are the limit.
[They go out through the gate. As they disappear
ZERO's grave opens suddenly and his head appears.]

ZERO

[Looking about]: That's funny! I thought I
heard her talkin' and laughin'. But I don't see nobody. Anyhow, what would she be doin' here? I
guess I must 'a' been dreamin'. But how could I be
dreamin' when I ain't been asleep? [He looks about
again]: Well, no use goin' back. I can't sleep, anyhow. I might as well walk around a little. [He rises
out of the ground, very rigidly. He wears a full-dress
suit of very antiquated cut and his hands are folded
stiffly across his breast.]

ZERO

[Walking woodenly]: Gee! I'm stiff! [He slowly
walks a few steps, then stops]: Gee, it's lonesome here!
[He shivers and walks on aimlessly]: I should 'a'

stayed where I was. But I thought I heard her laughin'.

[*A loud sneeze is heard.* ZERO *stands motionless, quaking with terror. The sneeze is repeated.*]

ZERO

[*Hoarsely*]: What's that?

A MILD VOICE

It's all right. Nothing to be afraid of.

[*From behind a headstone* SHRDLU *appears. He is dressed in a shabby and ill-fitting cutaway. He wears silver-rimmed spectacles and is smoking a cigarette.*]

SHRDLU

I hope I didn't frighten you.

ZERO

[*Still badly shaken*]: No-o. It's all right. You see, I wasn't expectin' to see anybody.

SHRDLU

You're a newcomer, aren't you?

ZERO

Yeh, this is my first night. I couldn't seem to get to sleep.

I can't sleep, eith
company, shall we?

[*Eagerly*]: Yeh,
in' awful lonesome.

[*Nodding*]: I kn
fortable.
[*He seats himself ea
follow his exampl
groans with pain.*

I'm kinda stiff.

You mustn't mind t
few days. [*He seats h
and produces a package
a Camel?*

No, I don't smoke.

I find it
a cigarett

[*Sudde
Do you m

No, go

[*Repla
catch you
[ZERO do

[*Mildly

I hear
scared if
off me.

[*Sadly
are as sn

Young Man

[*Half hysterically*]: What's that?

Judy

It's only the cats. They seem to like it here all right. But come on if you're afraid. [*They go toward the gate. As they go out*]: You nervous men sure are the limit.

[*They go out through the gate. As they disappear ZERO's grave opens suddenly and his head appears.*]

Zero

[*Looking about*]: That's funny! I thought I heard her talkin' and laughin'. But I don't see nobody. Anyhow, what would she be doin' here? I guess I must 'a' been dreamin'. But how could I be dreamin' when I ain't been asleep? [*He looks about again*]: Well, no use goin' back. I can't sleep, anyhow. I might as well walk around a little. [*He rises out of the ground, very rigidly. He wears a full-dress suit of very antiquated cut and his hands are folded stiffly across his breast.*]

Zero

[*Walking woodenly*]: Gee! I'm stiff! [*He slowly walks a few steps, then stops*]: Gee, it's lonesome here! [*He shivers and walks on aimlessly*]: I should 'a' stayed where I was. But I thought I heard her laughin'.

[*A loud sneeze is heard.* ZERO *stands motionless, quaking with terror. The sneeze is repeated.*]

ZERO

[*Hoarsely*]: What's that?

A MILD VOICE

It's all right. Nothing to be afraid of.

[*From behind a headstone* SHRDLU *appears. He is dressed in a shabby and ill-fitting cutaway. He wears silver-rimmed spectacles and is smoking a cigarette.*]

SHRDLU

I hope I didn't frighten you.

ZERO

[*Still badly shaken*]: No-o. It's all right. You see, I wasn't expectin' to see anybody.

SHRDLU

You're a newcomer, aren't you?

ZERO

Yeh, this is my first night. I couldn't seem to get to sleep.

Shrdlu

I can't sleep, either. Suppose we keep each other company, shall we?

Zero

[*Eagerly*]: Yeh, that would be great. I been feelin' awful lonesome.

Shrdlu

[*Nodding*]: I know. Let's make ourselves comfortable.

[*He seats himself easily on a grave. Zero tries to follow his example but he is stiff in every joint and groans with pain.*]

Zero

I'm kinda stiff.

Shrdlu

You mustn't mind the stiffness. It wears off in a few days. [*He seats himself on the grave beside Zero and produces a package of cigarettes.*] Will you have a Camel?

Zero

No, I don't smoke.

SHRDLU

I find it helps keep the mosquitoes away. [*He lights a cigarette.*]

SHRDLU

[*Suddenly taking the cigarette out of his mouth*]: Do you mind if I smoke, Mr.—Mr.——?

ZERO

No, go right ahead.

SHRDLU

[*Replacing the cigarette*]: Thank you. I didn't catch your name.
[ZERO *does not reply.*]

SHRDLU

[*Mildly*]: I say I didn't catch your name.

ZERO

I heard you the first time. [*Hesitantly*]: I'm scared if I tell you who I am and what I done, you'll be off me.

SHRDLU

[*Sadly*]: No matter what your sins may be, they are as snow compared to mine.

ZERO

You got another guess comin'. [*He pauses dramatically*]: My name's Zero. I'm a murderer.

SHRDLU

[*Nodding calmly*]: Oh, yes, I remember reading about you, Mr. Zero.

ZERO

[*A little piqued*]: And you still think you're worse than me?

SHRDLU

[*Throwing away his cigarette*]: Oh, a thousand times worse, Mr. Zero—a million times worse.

ZERO

What did you do?

SHRDLU

I, too, am a murderer.

ZERO

[*Looking at him in amazement*]: Go on! You're kiddin' me!

Shrdlu

Every word I speak is the truth, Mr. Zero. I am
the foulest, the most sinful of murderers! You only
murdered your employer, Mr. Zero. But I—I murdered my mother. [*He covers his face with his hands
and sobs.*]

Zero

[*Horrified*]: The hell yer say!

Shrdlu

[*Sobbing*]: Yes, my mother!—my beloved mother!

Zero

[*Suddenly*]: Say, you don't mean to say you're
Mr. ——

Shrdlu

[*Nodding*]: Yes. [*He wipes his eyes, still quivering with emotion.*]

Zero

I remember readin' about you in the papers.

Shrdlu

Yes, my guilt has been proclaimed to all the world.
But that would be a trifle if only I could wash the
stain of sin from my soul.

ZERO

I never heard of a guy killin' his mother before. What did you do it for?

SHRDLU

Because I have a sinful heart—there is no other reason.

ZERO

Did she always treat you square and all like that?

SHRDLU

She was a saint—a saint, I tell you. She cared for 'me and watched over me as only a mother can.

ZERO

You mean to say you didn't have a scrap or nothin'?

SHRDLU

Never a harsh or an unkind word. Nothing except loving care and good advice. From my infancy she devoted herself to guiding me on the right path. She taught me to be thrifty, to be devout, to be unselfish, to shun evil companions and to shut my ears to all the temptations of the flesh—in short, to become a virtuous, respectable, and God-fearing man. [*He groans*]: But it was a hopeless task. At fourteen I began to show evidence of my sinful nature.

ZERO

[*Breathlessly*]: You didn't kill anybody else, did you?

SHRDLU

No, thank God, there is only one murder on my soul. But I ran away from home.

ZERO

You did!

SHRDLU

Yes. A companion lent me a profane book—the only profane book I have ever read, I'm thankful to say. It was called "Treasure Island." Have you ever read it?

ZERO

No, I never was much on readin' books.

SHRDLU

It is a wicked book—a lurid tale of adventure. But it kindled in my sinful heart a desire to go to sea. And so I ran away from home.

ZERO

What did you do—get a job as a sailor?

SHRDLU

I never saw the sea—not to the day of my death. Luckily, my mother's loving intuition warned her of my intention and I was sent back home. She welcomed me with open arms. Not an angry word, not a look of reproach. But I could read the mute suffering in her eyes as we prayed together all through the night.

ZERO

[*Sympathetically*]: Gee, that must 'a' been tough. Gee, the mosquitoes are bad, ain't they? [*He tries awkwardly to slap at them with his stiff hands.*]

SHRDLU

[*Absorbed in his narrative*]: I thought that experience had cured me of evil and I began to think about a career. I wanted to go in foreign missions at first, but we couldn't bear the thought of the separation. So we finally decided that I should become a proof-reader.

ZERO

Say, slip me one o' them Camels, will you? I'm gettin' all bit up.

SHRDLU

Certainly. [*He hands ZERO cigarettes and matches.*]

Zero

[*Lighting up*]: Go ahead. I'm listenin'.

Shrdlu

By the time I was twenty I had a good job reading proof for a firm that printed catalogues. After a year they promoted me and let me specialize in shoe catalogues.

Zero

Yeh? That must 'a' been a good job.

Shrdlu

It was a very good job. I was on the shoe catalogues for thirteen years. I'd been on them yet, if I hadn't—— [*He chokes back a sob.*]

Zero

They oughta put a shot o' citronella in that embalmin'-fluid.

Shrdlu

[*He sighs*]: We were so happy together. I had my steady job. And Sundays we would go to morning, afternoon, and evening service. It was an honest and moral mode of life.

ZERO

It sure was.

SHRDLU

Then came that fatal Sunday. Dr. Amaranth, our minister, was having dinner with us—one of the few pure spirits on earth. When he had finished saying grace, we had our soup. Everything was going along as usual—we were eating our soup and discussing the sermon, just like every other Sunday I could remember. Then came the leg of lamb—— [*He breaks off, then resumes in a choking voice*]: I see the whole scene before me so plainly—it never leaves me—Dr. Amaranth at my right, my mother at my left, the leg of lamb on the table in front of me and the cuckoo clock on the little shelf between the windows. [*He stops and wipes his eyes.*]

ZERO

Yeh, but what happened?

SHRDLU

Well, as I started to carve the lamb—— Did you ever carve a leg of lamb?

ZERO

No, corned beef was our speed.

SHRDLU

It's very difficult on account of the bone. And when there's gravy in the dish there's danger of spilling it. So Mother always used to hold the dish for me. She leaned forward, just as she always did, and I could see the gold locket around her neck. It had my picture in it and one of my baby curls. Well, I raised my knife to carve the leg of lamb—and instead I cut my mother's throat! [*He sobs.*]

ZERO

You must 'a' been crazy!

SHRDLU

[*Raising his head, vehemently*]: No! Don't try to justify me. I wasn't crazy. They tried to prove at the trial that I was crazy. But Dr. Amaranth saw the truth! He saw it from the first! He knew that it was my sinful nature—and he told me what was in store for me.

ZERO

[*Trying to be comforting*]: Well, your troubles are over now.

SHRDLU

[*His voice rising*]: Over! Do you think this is the end?

ZERO

Sure. What more can they do to us?

SHRDLU

[*His tones growing shriller and shriller*]: Do you think there can ever be any peace for such as we are—murderers, sinners? Don't you know what awaits us—flames, eternal flames!

ZERO

[*Nervously*]: Keep your shirt on, Buddy—they wouldn't do that to us.

SHRDLU

There's no escape—no escape for us, I tell you. We're doomed! We're doomed to suffer unspeakable torments through all eternity. [*His voice rises higher and higher.*]

[*A grave opens suddenly and a head appears.*]

THE HEAD

Hey, you birds! Can't you shut up and let a guy sleep?

[*ZERO scrambles painfully to his feet.*]

ZERO

[*To SHRDLU*]: Hey, put on the soft pedal.

SHEDLU

[*Too wrought up to attend*]: It won't be long now! We'll receive our summons soon.

THE HEAD

Are you goin' to beat it or not? [*He calls into the grave*]: Hey, Bill, lend me your head a minute. [*A moment later his arm appears holding a skull.*]

ZERO

[*Warningly*]: Look out! [*He seizes* SHEDLU *and drags him away just as* THE HEAD *throws the skull.*]

THE HEAD

[*Disgustedly*]: Missed 'em. Damn old tabby cats! I'll get 'em next time. [*A prodigious yawn*]: Ho-hum! Me for the worms!
[THE HEAD *disappears as the curtain falls.*]

SCENE SIX

[*SCENE: A pleasant place. A scene of pastoral loveliness. A meadow dotted with fine old trees and carpeted with rich grass and field flowers. In the background are seen a number of tents fashioned of gay-striped silks and beyond gleams a meandering river. Clear air and a fleckless sky. Sweet distant music throughout.*

At the rise of the curtain, SHEDLU *is seen seated under a tree in the foreground in an attitude of deep dejection. His knees are drawn up and his head is buried in his arms. He is dressed as in the preceding scene.*

A few minutes later, ZERO *enters at right. He walks slowly and looks about him with an air of half-suspicious curiosity. He, too, is dressed as in the preceding scene. Suddenly he sees* SHEDLU *seated under the tree. He stands still and looks at him half fearfully. Then, seeing something familiar in him, goes closer.* SHEDLU *is unaware of his presence. At last* ZERO *recognizes him and grins in pleased surprise.*]

ZERO

Well, if it ain't——! [*He claps* SHEDLU *on the shoulder*]: Hello, Buddy!

[SHRDLU *looks up slowly, then recognizing* ZERO, *he rises gravely and extends his hand courteously*.]

SHRDLU

How do you do, Mr. Zero? I'm very glad to see you again.

ZERO

Same here. I wasn't expectin' to see you, either. [*Looking about*]: This is a kinda nice place. I wouldn't mind restin' here a while.

SHRDLU

You may if you wish.

ZERO

I'm kinda tired. I ain't used to bein' outdoors. I ain't walked so much in years.

SHRDLU

Sit down here, under the tree.

ZERO

Do they let you sit on the grass?

SHRDLU

Oh, yes.

Zero

[*Seating himself*]: Boy, this feels good. I'll tell the world my feet are sore. I ain't used to so much walkin'. Say, I wonder would it be all right if I took my shoes off; my feet are tired.

Shrdlu

Yes. Some of the people here go barefoot.

Zero

Yeh? They sure must be nuts. But I'm goin' t' leave 'em off for a while. So long as it's all right. The grass feels nice and cool. [*He stretches out comfortably*]: Say, this is the life of Riley all right, all right. This sure is a nice place. What do they call this place, anyhow?

Shrdlu

The Elysian Fields.

Zero

The which?

Shrdlu

The Elysian Fields.

Zero

[*Dubiously*]: Oh! Well, it's a nice place, all right.

Shrdlu

They say that this is the most desirable of all places. Only the most favoured remain here.

Zero

Yeh? Well, that let's me out, I guess. [*Suddenly*]: But what are you doin' here? I thought you'd be burned by now.

Shrdlu

[*Sadly*]: Mr. Zero, I am the most unhappy of men.

Zero

[*In mild astonishment*]: Why, because you ain't bein' roasted alive?

Shrdlu

[*Nodding*]: Nothing is turning out as I expected. I saw everything so clearly—the flames, the tortures, an eternity of suffering as the just punishment for my unspeakable crime. And it has all turned out so differently.

Zero

Well, that's pretty soft for you, ain't it?

Shrdlu

[*Wailingly*]: No, no, no! It's right and just that I should be punished. I could have endured it stoically. All through those endless ages of indescribable torment I should have exulted in the magnificence of divine justice. But this—this is maddening! What becomes of justice? What becomes of morality? What becomes of right and wrong? It's maddening —simply maddening! Oh, if Dr. Amaranth were only here to advise me! [*He buries his face and groans.*]

Zero

[*Trying to puzzle it out*]: You mean to say they ain't called you for cuttin' your mother's throat?

Shrdlu

No! It's terrible—terrible! I was prepared for anything—anything but this.

Zero

Well, what did they say to you?

Shrdlu

[*Looking up*]: Only that I was to come here and remain until I understood.

Zero

I don't get it. What do they want you to understand?

Shrdlu

[*Despairingly*]: I don't know—I don't know! If I only had an inkling of what they meant—— [*Interrupting him*]: Just listen quietly for a moment; do you hear anything?

[*They are both silent, straining their ears.*]

Zero

[*At length*]: Nope.

Shrdlu

You don't hear any music? Do you?

Zero

Music? No, I don't hear nothin'.

Shrdlu

The people here say that the music never stops.

Zero

They're kiddin' you.

Shrdlu

Do you think so?

ZERO

Sure thing.   There ain't a sound.

SHRDLU

Perhaps.   They're capable of anything.   But I haven't told you of the bitterest of my disappointments.

ZERO

Well, spill it.   I'm gettin' used to hearin' bad news.

SHRDLU

When I came to this place, my first thought was to find my dear mother.   I wanted to ask her forgiveness. And I wanted her to help me to understand.

ZERO

An' she couldn't do it?

SHRDLU

[*With a deep groan*]:   She's not here!   Mr. Zero! Here where only the most favoured dwell, that wisest and purest of spirits is nowhere to be found.   I don't understand it.

A WOMAN'S VOICE

[*In the distance*]:   Mr. Zero!   Oh, Mr. Zero! [*ZERO raises his head and listens attentively.*]

SHRDLU

[*Going on, unheedingly*]: If you were to see some of the people here—the things they do——

ZERO

[*Interrupting*]: Wait a minute, will you? I think somebody's callin' me.

THE VOICE

[*Somewhat nearer*]: Mr. Ze-ro! Oh! Mr. Ze-ro!

ZERO

Who the hell's that now? I wonder if the wife's on my trail already. That would be swell, wouldn't it? An' I figured on her bein' good for another twenty years, anyhow.

THE VOICE

[*Nearer*]: Mr. Ze-ro! Yoo-hoo!

ZERO

No. That ain't her voice. [*Calling, savagely*]: Yoo-hoo. [*To* SHRDLU]: Ain't that always the way? Just when a guy is takin' life easy an' havin' a good time! [*He rises and looks off left*]: Here she comes, whoever she is. [*In sudden amazement*]: Well, I'll be——! Well, what do you know about that!

[*He stands looking in wonderment, as* DAISY DIANA
   DOROTHEA DEVORE *enters. She wears a much-
   beruffled white muslin dress which is a size too
   small and fifteen years too youthful for her. She
   is red-faced and breathless.*]

DAISY

[*Panting*]: Oh! I thought I'd never catch up to
you. I've been followin' you for days—callin' an'
callin'. Didn't you hear me?

ZERO

Not till just now. You look kinda winded.

DAISY

I sure am. I can't hardly catch my breath.

ZERO

Well, sit down an' take a load off your feet. [*He
leads her to the tree.*]
[DAISY *sees* SHRDLU *for the first time and shrinks back
   a little.*]

ZERO

It's all right, he's a friend of mine. [*To* SHRDLU]:
Buddy, I want you to meet my friend, Miss Devore.

Shedlu

[*Rising and extending his hand courteously*]:   How do you do, Miss Devore?

Daisy

[*Self-consciously*]:   How do!

Zero

[*To* Daisy]:   He's a friend of mine.   [*To* Shedlu]: I guess you don't mind if she sits here a while an' cools off, do you?

Shedlu

No, no, certainly not.

[*They all seat themselves under the tree.   Zero and Daisy are a little self-conscious.   Shedlu gradually becomes absorbed in his own thoughts.*]

Zero

I was just takin' a rest myself.   I took my shoes off on account of my feet bein' so sore.

Daisy

Yeh, I'm kinda tired, too.   [*Looking about*]:   Say, ain't it pretty here, though?

Zero

Yeh, it is at that.

DAISY

What do they call this place?

ZERO

Why—er—let's see. He was tellin' me just a minute ago. The—er—I don't know. Some kind o' fields. I forget now. [*To* SHRDLU]: Say, Buddy, what do they call this place again? [SHRDLU, *absorbed in his thoughts, does not hear him. To* DAISY]: He don't hear me. He's thinkin' again.

DAISY

[*Sotto voce*]: What's the matter with him?

ZERO

Why, he's the guy that murdered his mother—remember?

DAISY

[*Interested*]: Oh, yeh! Is that him?

ZERO

Yeh. An' he had it all figgered out how they was goin' t' roast him or somethin'. And now they ain't goin' to do nothin' to him an' it's kinda got his goat.

DAISY

[*Sympathetically*]: Poor feller!

Zero

Yeh. He takes it kinda hard.

Daisy

He looks like a nice young feller.

Zero

Well, you sure are good for sore eyes. I never expected to see you here.

Daisy

I thought maybe you'd be kinda surprised.

Zero

Surprised is right. I thought you was alive an' kickin'. When did you pass out?

Daisy

Oh, right after you did—a coupla days.

Zero

[*Interested*]: Yeh? What happened? Get hit by a truck or somethin'?

Daisy

No. [*Hesitantly*]: You see—it's this way. I blew out the gas.

ZERO

[*Astonished*]: Go on! What was the big idea?

DAISY

[*Falteringly*]: Oh, I don't know. You see, I lost my job.

ZERO

I'll bet you're sorry you did it now, ain't you?

DAISY

[*With conviction*]: No, I ain't sorry. Not a bit. [*Then hesitantly*]: Say, Mr. Zero, I been thinkin'—— [*She stops.*]

ZERO

What?

DAISY

[*Plucking up courage*]: I been thinkin' it would be kinda nice—if you an' me—if we could kinda talk things over.

ZERO

Yeh. Sure. What do you want to talk about?

DAISY

Well—I don't know—but you and me—we ain't really ever talked things over, have we?

Zero

No, that's right, we ain't. Well, let's go to it.

Daisy

I was thinkin' if we could be alone—just the two of us, see?

Zero

Oh, yeh! Yeh, I get you. [*He turns to* Shrdlu *and coughs loudly.* Shrdlu *does not stir.*]

Zero

[*To* Daisy]: He's dead to the world. [*He turns to* Shrdlu]: Say, Buddy! [*No answer*]: Say, Buddy!

Shrdlu

[*Looking up with a start*]: Were you speaking to me?

Zero

Yeh. How'd you guess it? I was thinkin' that maybe you'd like to walk around a little and look for your mother.

Shrdlu

[*Shaking his head*]: It's no use. I've looked everywhere. [*He relapses into thought again.*]

Zero

Maybe over there they might know.

Shrdlu

No, no! I've searched everywhere. She's not here. [*Zero and Daisy look at each other in despair.*]

Zero

Listen, old shirt, my friend here and me—see?—we used to work in the same store. An' we got some things to talk over—business, see?—kinda confidential. So if it ain't askin' too much——

Shrdlu

[*Springing to his feet*]: Why, certainly! Excuse me!

[*He bows politely to Daisy and walks off. Daisy and Zero watch him until he has disappeared.*]

Zero

[*With a forced laugh*]: He's a good guy at that.

[*Now that they are alone, both are very self-conscious, and for a time they sit in silence.*]

Daisy

[*Breaking the silence*]: It sure is pretty here, ain't it?

ZERO

Sure is.

DAISY

Look at the flowers! Ain't they just perfect! Why, you'd think they was artificial, wouldn't you?

ZERO

Yeh, you would.

DAISY

And the smell of them.   Like perfume.

ZERO

Yeh.

DAISY

I'm crazy about the country, ain't you?

ZERO

Yeh.   It's nice for a change.

DAISY

Them store picnics—remember?

ZERO

You bet.   They sure was fun.

DAISY

One time—I guess you don't remember—the two of us—me and you—we sat down on the grass together under a tree—just like we're doin' now.

ZERO

Sure I remember.

DAISY

Go on! I'll bet you don't.

ZERO

I'll bet I do. It was the year the wife didn't go.

DAISY

[*Her face brightening*]: That's right! I didn't think you'd remember.

ZERO

An' comin' home we sat together in the truck.

DAISY

[*Eagerly, rather shamefacedly*]: Yeh! There's somethin' I've always wanted to ask you.

ZERO

Well, why didn't you?

Daisy

I don't know. It didn't seem refined. But I'm goin' to ask you now, anyhow.

Zero

Go ahead. Shoot.

Daisy

[*Falteringly*]: Well—while we was comin' home—you put your arm up on the bench behind me—and I could feel your knee kinda pressin' against mine. [*She stops.*]

Zero

[*Becoming more and more interested*]: Yeh—well —what about it?

Daisy

What I wanted to ask you was—was it just kinda accidental?

Zero

[*With a laugh*]: Sure it was accidental. Accidental on purpose.

Daisy

[*Eagerly*]: Do you mean it?

ZERO

Sure I mean it.   You mean to say you didn't know it?

DAISY

No.   I've been wantin' to ask you——

ZERO

Then why did you get sore at me?

DAISY

Sore?   I wasn't sore!   When was I sore?

ZERO

That night.   Sure you was sore.   If you wasn't sore why did you move away?

DAISY

Just to see if you meant it.   I thought if you meant it you'd move up closer.   An' then when you took your arm away I was sure you didn't mean it.

ZERO

An' I thought all the time you was sore.   That's why I took my arm away.   I thought if I moved up you'd holler and then I'd be in a jam, like you read in the paper all the time about guys gettin' pulled in for annoyin' women.

DAISY

An' I was wishin' you'd put your arm around me—just sittin' there wishin' all the way home.

ZERO

What do you know about that? That sure is hard luck, that is. If I'd 'a' only knew! You know what I felt like doin'—only I didn't have the nerve?

DAISY

What?

ZERO

I felt like kissin' you.

DAISY

[*Fervently*]: I wanted you to.

ZERO

[*Astonished*]: You would 'a' let me?

DAISY

I wanted you to! I wanted you to! Oh, why didn't you—why didn't you?

ZERO

I didn't have the nerve. I sure was a dumb-bell.

DAISY

I would 'a' let you all you wanted to. I wouldn't 'a' cared. I know it would 'a' been wrong but I wouldn't 'a' cared. I wasn't thinkin' about right an' wrong at all. I didn't care—see? I just wanted you to kiss me.

ZERO

[*Feelingly*]: If I'd only knew. I wanted to do it, I swear I did. But I didn't think you cared nothin' about me.

DAISY

[*Passionately*]: I never cared nothin' about nobody else.

ZERO

Do you mean it—on the level? You ain't kiddin' me, are you?

DAISY

No, I ain't kiddin'. I mean it. I'm tellin' you the truth. I ain't never had the nerve to tell you before —but now I don't care. It don't make no difference now. I mean it—every word of it.

ZERO

[*Dejectedly*]: If I'd only knew it.

DAISY

Listen to me.   There's somethin' else I want to tell you.   I may as well tell you everything now.   It don't make no difference now.   About my blowin' out the gas—see?   Do you know why I done it?

ZERO

Yeh, you told me—on account o' bein' canned.

DAISY

I just told you that.   That ain't the real reason. The real reason is on account o' you.

ZERO

You mean to say on account o' me passin' out——?

DAISY

Yeh.   That's it.   I didn't want to go on livin'. What for?   What did I want to go on livin' for?   I didn't have nothin' to live for with you gone.   I often thought of doin' it before.   But I never had the nerve. An' anyhow I didn't want to leave you.

ZERO

An' me bawlin' you out, about readin' too fast an' readin' too slow.

DAISY

[*Reproachfully*]: Why did you do it?

ZERO

I don't know, I swear I don't. I was always stuck on you. An' while I'd be addin' them figgers, I'd be thinkin' how if the wife died, you an' me could get married.

DAISY

I used to think o' that, too.

ZERO

An' then before I knew it, I was bawlin' you out.

DAISY

Them was the times I'd think o' blowin' out the gas. But I never did till you was gone. There wasn't nothin' to live for then. But it wasn't so easy to do, anyhow. I never could stand the smell o' gas. An' all the while I was gettin' ready, you know, stuffin' up all the cracks, the way you read about in the paper— I was thinkin' of you and hopin' that maybe I'd meet you again. An' I made up my mind if I ever did see you, I'd tell you.

ZERO

[*Taking her hand*]: I'm sure glad you did. I'm sure glad. [*Ruefully*]: But it don't do much good now, does it?

DAISY

No, I guess it don't. [*Summoning courage.*] But there's one thing I'm goin' to ask you.

ZERO

What's that?

DAISY

[*In a low voice*]: I want you to kiss me.

ZERO

You bet I will! [*He leans over and kisses her cheek*].

DAISY

Not like that. I don't mean like that. I mean really kiss me. On the mouth. I ain't never been kissed like that.

[ZERO *puts his arms about her and presses his lips to hers. A long embrace. At last they separate and sit side by side in silence.*]

DAISY

[*Putting her hands to her cheeks*]: So that's what it's like. I didn't know it could be like that. I didn't know anythin' could be like that.

ZERO

[*Fondling her hand*]: Your cheeks are red. They're all red. And your eyes are shinin'. I never seen your eyes shinin' like that before.

DAISY

[*Holding up her hand*]: Listen—do you hear it? Do you hear the music?

ZERO

No, I don't hear nothin'!

DAISY

Yeh—music. Listen an' you'll hear it.
[*They are both silent for a moment.*]

ZERO

[*Excitedly*]: Yeh! I hear it! He said there was music, but I didn't hear it till just now.

DAISY

Ain't it grand?

ZERO

Swell! Say, do you know what?

DAISY

What?

ZERO

It makes me feel like dancin'.

DAISY

Yeh? Me, too.

ZERO

[*Springing to his feet*]: Come on! Let's dance!
[*He seizes her hands and tries to pull her up.*]

DAISY

[*Resisting laughingly*]: I can't dance. I ain't
danced in twenty years.

ZERO

That's nothin'. I ain't, neither. Come on! I feel
just like a kid!
[*He pulls her to her feet and seizes her about the
waist.*]

DAISY

Wait a minute! Wait till I fix my skirt.

[*She turns back her skirts and pins them above the ankles.*]

[Zero *seizes her about the waist. They dance clum-sily but with gay abandon.* Daisy's *hair becomes loosened and tumbles over her shoulders. She lends herself more and more to the spirit of the dance. But* Zero *soon begins to tire and dances with less and less zest.*]

Zero

[*Stopping at last, panting for breath*]: Wait a minute! I'm all winded.

[*He releases* Daisy, *but before he can turn away, she throws her arms about him and presses her lips to his.*

Zero

[*Freeing himself*]: Wait a minute! Let me get my wind!

[*He limps to the tree and seats himself under it, gasp-ing for breath.* Daisy *looks after him, her spirits rather dampened.*]

Zero

Whew! I sure am winded! I ain't used to dancin'.

[*He takes off his collar and tie and opens the neck-band of his shirt.* Daisy *sits under the tree near*

*him, looking at him longingly.   But he is busy
catching his breath.*]
Gee, my heart's goin' a mile a minute.

DAISY

Why don't you lay down an' rest?   You could put
your head on my lap.

ZERO

That ain't a bad idea.
[*He stretches out, his head in DAISY's lap.*]

DAISY

[*Fondling his hair*]:   It was swell, wasn't it?

ZERO

Yeh.   But you gotta be used to it.

DAISY

Just imagine if we could stay here all the time—you
an' me together—wouldn't it be swell?

ZERO

Yeh.   But there ain't a chance.

DAISY

Won't they let us stay?

ZERO

No. This place is only for the good ones.

DAISY

Well, we ain't so bad, are we?

ZERO

Go on! Me a murderer an' you committin' suicide. Anyway, they wouldn't stand for this—the way we been goin' on.

DAISY

I don't see why.

ZERO

You don't! You know it ain't right. Ain't I got a wife?

DAISY

Not any more you ain't. When you're dead that ends it. Don't they always say "until death do us part?"

ZERO

Well, maybe you're right about that but they wouldn't stand for us here.

DAISY

It would be swell—the two of us together—we could make up for all them years.

ZERO

Yeh, I wish we could.

DAISY

We sure were fools. But I don't care. I've got you now. [*She kisses his forehead and cheeks and mouth.*]

ZERO

I'm sure crazy about you. I never saw you lookin' so pretty before, with your cheeks all red. An' your hair hangin' down. You got swell hair. [*He fondles and kisses her hair.*]

DAISY

[*Ecstatically*]: We got each other now, ain't we?

ZERO

Yeh. I'm crazy about you. Daisy! That's a pretty name. It's a flower, ain't it? Well—that's what you are—just a flower.

DAISY

[*Happily*]: We can always be together now, can't we?

ZERO

As long as they'll let us.   I sure am crazy about
you.   [*Suddenly he sits upright*]:   Watch your step!

DAISY

[*Alarmed*]:   What's the matter?

ZERO

[*Nervously*]:   He's comin' back.

DAISY

Oh, is that all?   Well, what about it?

ZERO

You don't want him to see us layin' around like this,
do you?

DAISY

I don't care if he does.

ZERO

Well, you oughta care.   You don't want him to
think you ain't a refined girl, do you?   He's an awful
moral bird, he is.

DAISY

I don't care nothin' about him.   I don't care nothin'
about anybody but you.

ZERO

Sure, I know. But we don't want people talkin'
about us. You better fix your hair an' pull down your
skirts.

[DAISY *complies rather sadly. They are both silent*
as SHRDLU *enters.*]

ZERO

[*With feigned nonchalance*]: Well, you got back
all right, didn't you?

SHRDLU

I hope I haven't returned too soon.

ZERO

No, that's all right. We were just havin' a little
talk. You know—about business an' things.

DAISY

[*Boldly*]: We were wishin' we could stay here all
the time.

SHRDLU

You may if you like.

ZERO AND DAISY

[*In astonishment*]: What!

SHRDLU

Yes.   Any one who likes may remain——

ZERO

But I thought you were tellin' me——

SHRDLU

Just as I told you, only the most favored do remain. But any one may.

ZERO

I don't get it.   There's a catch in it somewheres.

DAISY

It don't matter as long as we can stay.

ZERO

[*To* SHRDLU]:   We were thinkin' about gettin' married, see?

SHRDLU

You may or not, just as you like.

ZERO

You don't mean to say we could stay if we didn't, do you?

SHRDLU

Yes.   They don't care.

Zero

An' there's some here that ain't married?

Shrdlu

Yes.

Zero

[*To* Daisy]: I don't know about this place, at that. They must be kind of a mixed crowd.

Daisy

It don't matter, so long as we got each other.

Zero

Yeh, I know, but you don't want to mix with people that ain't respectable.

Daisy

[*To* Shrdlu]: Can we get married right away? I guess there must be a lot of ministers here, ain't there?

Shrdlu

Not as many as I had hoped to find. The two who seem most beloved are Dean Swift and the Abbé Rabelais. They are both much admired for some indecent tales which they have written.

Zero

[*Shocked*]: What! Ministers writin' smutty stories! Say, what kind of a dump is this, anyway?

Shrdlu

[*Despairingly*]: I don't know, Mr. Zero. All these people here are so strange, so unlike the good people I've known. They seem to think of nothing but enjoyment or of wasting their time in profitless occupations. Some paint pictures from morning until night, or carve blocks of stone. Others write songs or put words together, day in and day out. Still others do nothing but lie under the trees and look at the sky. There are men who spend all their time reading books and women who think only of adorning themselves. And forever they are telling stories and laughing and singing and drinking and dancing. There are drunkards, thieves, vagabonds, blasphemers, adulterers. There is one——

Zero

That's enough. I heard enough. [*He seats himself and begins putting on his shoes.*]

Daisy

[*Anxiously*]: What are you goin' to do?

Zero

I'm goin' to beat it, that's what I'm goin' to do.

DAISY

You said you liked it here.

ZERO

[*Looking at her in amazement*]: Liked it! Say, you don't mean to say you want to stay here, do you, with a lot of rummies an' loafers an' bums?

DAISY

We don't have to bother with them. We can just sit here together an' look at the flowers an' listen to the music.

SHRDLU

[*Eagerly*]: Music! Did you hear music?

DAISY

Sure. Don't you hear it?

SHRDLU

No, they say it never stops. But I've never heard it.

ZERO

[*Listening*]: I thought I heard it before but I don't hear nothin' now. I guess I must 'a' been dreamin'. [*Looking about*]: What's the quickest way out of this place?

DAISY

[*Pleadingly*]:   Won't you stay just a little longer?

ZERO

Didn't yer hear me say I'm goin'?   Good-bye, Miss
Devore.   I'm goin' to beat it.
[*He limps off at the right.*   DAISY *follows him slowly.*]

DAISY

[*To* SHEDLU]:   I won't ever see him again.

SHEDLU

Are you goin' to stay here?

DAISY

It don't make no difference now.   Without him I
might as well be alive.
[*She goes off right.*   SHEDLU *watches her a moment,
then sighs and seating himself under the tree,
buries his head on his arm.   Curtain falls.*]

SCENE SEVEN

[*SCENE: Before the curtain rises the clicking of an adding machine is heard. The curtain rises upon an office similar in appearance to that in* SCENE TWO *except that there is a door in the back wall through which can be seen a glimpse of the corridor outside. In the middle of the room* ZERO *is seated completely absorbed in the operation of an adding machine. He presses the keys and pulls the lever with mechanical precision. He still wears his full-dress suit but he has added to it sleeve protectors and a green eye shade. A strip of white paper-tape flows steadily from the machine as* ZERO *operates. The room is filled with this tape—streamers, festoons, billows of it everywhere. It covers the floor and the furniture, it climbs the walls and chokes the doorways. A few moments later,* LIEUTENANT CHARLES *and* JOE *enter at the left.* LIEUTENANT CHARLES *is middle-aged and inclined to corpulence. He has an air of world-weariness. He is bare-footed, wears a Panama hat, and is dressed in bright red tights which are a very bad fit— too tight in some places, badly wrinkled in others.* JOE *is a youth with a smutty face dressed in dirty blue overalls.*]

Charles

[*After contemplating* Zero *for a few moments*]:
All right, Zero, cease firing.

Zero

[*Looking up, surprised*]: Whaddja say?

Charles

I said stop punching that machine.

Zero

[*Bewildered*]: Stop? [*He goes on working mechanically.*]

Charles

[*Impatiently*]: Yes. Can't you stop? Here, Joe, give me a hand. He can't stop.
[Joe *and* Charles *each take one of* Zero's *arms and with enormous effort detach him from the machine. He resists passively—mere inertia. Finally they succeed and swing him around on his stool.* Charles *and* Joe *mop their foreheads.*]

Zero

[*Querulously*]: What's the idea? Can't you lemme alone?

CHARLES

[*Ignoring the question*]: How long have you been here?

ZERO

Jes' twenty-five years. Three hundred months, ninety-one hundred and thirty-one days, one hundred thirty-six thousand——

CHARLES

[*Impatiently*]: That'll do! That'll do!

ZERO

[*Proudly*]: I ain't missed a day, not an hour, not a minute. Look at all I got done. [*He points to the maze of paper.*]

CHARLES

It's time to quit.

ZERO

Quit? Whaddye mean quit? I ain't goin' to quit!

CHARLES

You've got to.

ZERO

What for? What do I have to quit for?

CHARLES

It's time for you to go back.

ZERO

Go back where? Whaddya talkin' about?

CHARLES

Back to earth, you dub. Where do you think?

ZERO

Aw, go on, Cap, who are you kiddin'?

CHARLES

I'm not kidding anybody. And don't call me Cap.
I'm a lieutenant.

ZERO

All right, Lieutenant, all right. But what's this
you're tryin' to tell me about goin' back?

CHARLES

Your time's up, I'm telling you. You must be
pretty thick. How many times do you want to be told
a thing?

ZERO

This is the first time I heard about goin' back. Nobody ever said nothin' to me about it before.

CHARLES

You didn't think you were going to stay here forever, did you?

ZERO

Sure. Why not? I did my bit, didn't I? Forty-five years of it. Twenty-five years in the store. Then the boss canned me and I knocked him cold. I guess you ain't heard about that——

CHARLES

[*Interrupting*]: I know all about that. But what's that got to do with it?

ZERO

Well, I done my bit, didn't I? That oughta let me out.

CHARLES

[*Jeeringly*]: So you think you're all through, do you?

ZERO

Sure, I do. I did the best I could while I was there and then I passed out. And now I'm sittin' pretty here.

Charles

You've got a fine idea of the way they run things, you have. Do you think they're going to all of the trouble of making a soul just to use it once?

Zero

Once is often enough, it seems to me.

Charles

It seems to you, does it? Well, who are you? And what do you know about it? Why, man, they use a soul over and over again—over and over until it's worn out.

Zero

Nobody ever told me.

Charles

So you thought you were all through, did you? Well, that's a hot one, that is.

Zero

[*Sullenly*]: How was I to know?

Charles

Use your brains! Where would we put them all? We're crowded enough as it is. Why, this place is nothing but a kind of repair and service station—a sort of cosmic laundry, you might say. We get the souls in here by the bushelful. Then we get busy and clean them up. And you ought to see some of them. The muck and the slime. Phoo! And as full of holes as a flour-sifter. But we fix them up. We disinfect them and give them a kerosene rub and mend the holes and back they go—practically as good as new.

Zero

You mean to say I've been here before—before the last time, I mean?

Charles

Been here before! Why, you poor boob—you've been here thousands of times—fifty thousand, at least.

Zero

[*Suspiciously*]: How is it I don't remember nothin' about it?

Charles

Well—that's partly because you're stupid. But it's mostly because that's the way they fix it. [*Musingly*]: They're funny that way—every now and then they'll do something white like that—when you'd least expect it. I guess economy's at the bottom of it, though. They figure that the souls would get worn out quicker if they remembered.

ZERO

And don't any of 'em remember?

CHARLES

Oh, some do. You see there's different types: there's the type that gets a little better each time it goes back—we just give them a wash and send them right through. Then there's another type—the type that gets a little worse each time. That's where you belong!

ZERO

[*Offended*]: Me? You mean to say I'm gettin' worse all the time?

CHARLES

[*Nodding*]: Yes. A little worse each time.

ZERO

Well—what was I when I started? Somethin' big? —A king or somethin'?

CHARLES

[*Laughing derisively*]: A king! That's a good one! I'll tell you what you were the first time—if you want to know so much—a monkey.

ZERO

[*Shocked and offended*]: A monkey!

CHARLES

[*Nodding*]: Yes, sir—just a hairy, chattering, long-tailed monkey.

ZERO

That musta been a long time ago.

CHARLES

Oh, not so long. A million years or so. Seems like yesterday to me.

ZERO

Then look here, whaddya mean by sayin' I'm gettin' worse all the time?

CHARLES

Just what I said. You weren't so bad as a monkey. Of course, you did just what all the other monkeys did, but still it kept you out in the open air. And you weren't women-shy—there was one little red-headed monkey—— Well, never mind. Yes, sir, you weren't so bad then. But even in those days there must have been some bigger and brainier monkey that you kow-towed to. The mark of the slave was on you from the start.

ZERO

[*Sullenly*]: You ain't very particular about what you call people, are you?

CHARLES

You wanted the truth, didn't you? If there ever was a soul in the world that was labelled slave it's yours. Why, all the bosses and kings that there ever were have left their trademarks on your backside.

ZERO

It ain't fair, if you ask me.

CHARLES

[*Shrugging his shoulders*]: Don't tell me about it. I don't make the rules. All I know is you've been getting worse—worse each time. Why, even six thousand years ago you weren't so bad. That was the time you were hauling stones for one of those big pyramids in a place they call Africa. Ever hear of the pyramids?

ZERO

Them big pointy things?

CHARLES

[*Nodding*]: That's it.

ZERO

I seen a picture of them in the movies.

CHARLES

Well, you helped build them. It was a long step down from the happy days in the jungle, but it was a good job—even though you didn't know what you were doing and your back was striped by the foreman's whip. But you've been going down, down. Two thousand years ago you were a Roman galley-slave. You were on one of the triremes that knocked the Carthaginian fleet for a goal. Again the whip. But you had muscles then—chest muscles, back muscles, biceps. [*He feels* ZERO's *arm gingerly and turns away in disgust*]: Phoo! A bunch of mush! [*He notices that* JOE *has fallen asleep. Walking over, he kicks him in the shin.*]

CHARLES

Wake up, you mutt! Where do you think you are! [*He turns to* ZERO *again*]: And then another thousand years and you were a serf—a lump of clay digging up other lumps of clay. You wore an iron collar then—white ones hadn't been invented yet. Another long step down. But where you dug, potatoes grew and that helped fatten the pigs. Which was something. And now—well, I don't want to rub it in——

ZERO

Rub it in is right! Seems to me I got a pretty healthy kick comin'. I ain't had a square deal! Hard work! That's all I've ever had!

CHARLES

[*Callously*]: What else were you ever good for?

ZERO

Well, that ain't the point. The point is I'm through! I had enough! Let 'em find somebody else to do the dirty work. I'm sick of bein' the goat! I quit right here and now! [*He glares about defiantly. There is a thunder-clap and a bright flash of lightning.*]

ZERO

[*Screaming*]: Ooh! What's that? [*He clings to* CHARLES.]

CHARLES

It's all right. Nobody's going to hurt you. It's just their way of telling you that they don't like you to talk that way. Pull yourself together and calm down. You can't change the rules—nobody can— they've got it all fixed. It's a rotten system—but what are you going to do about it?

Zero

Why can't they stop pickin' on me? I'm satisfied here—doin' my day's work. I don't want to go back.

Charles

You've got to, I tell you. There's no way out of it.

Zero

What chance have I got—at my age? Who'll give me a job?

Charles

You big boob, you don't think you're going back the way you are, do you?

Zero

Sure, how then?

Charles

Why, you've got to start all over.

Zero

All over?

Charles

[*Nodding*]: You'll be a baby again—a bald, red-faced little animal, and then you'll go through it all again. There'll be millions of others like you—all with their mouths open, squalling for food. And then when you get a little older you'll begin to learn things —and you'll learn all the wrong things and learn them all in the wrong way. You'll eat the wrong food and wear the wrong clothes and you'll live in swarming dens where there's no light and no air! You'll learn to be a liar and a bully and a braggart and a coward and a sneak. You'll learn to fear the sunlight and to hate beauty. By that time you'll be ready for school. There they'll tell you the truth about a great many things that you don't give a damn about and they'll tell you lies about all the things you ought to know— and about all the things you want to know they'll tell you nothing at all. When you get through you'll be equipped for your life-work. You'll be ready to take a job.

Zero

[*Eagerly*]: What'll my job be? Another adding machine?

Charles

Yes. But not one of these antiquated adding machines. It will be a superb, super-hyper-adding machine, as far from this old piece of junk as you are from God. It will be something to make you sit up and take notice, that adding machine. It will be an adding machine which will be installed in a coal mine and which will record the individual output of each miner. As each miner down in the lower galleries takes up a shovelful of coal, the impact of his shovel will automatically set in motion a graphite pencil in your gallery. The pencil will make a mark in white upon a blackened, sensitized drum. Then your work comes in. With the great toe of your right foot you release a lever which focuses a violet ray on the drum. The ray playing upon and through the white mark, falls upon a selenium cell which in turn sets the keys of the adding apparatus in motion. In this way the individual output of each miner is recorded without any human effort except the slight pressure of the great toe of your right foot.

ZERO

[*In breathless, round-eyed wonder*]: Say, that'll be some machine, won't it?

CHARLES

Some machine is right. It will be the culmination of human effort—the final triumph of the evolutionary process. For millions of years the nebulous gases swirled in space. For more millions of years the gases cooled and then through inconceivable ages they hardened into rocks. And then came life. Floating green things on the waters that covered the earth. More millions of years and a step upward—an animate organism in the ancient slime. And so on—step by step, down through the ages—a gain here, a gain there—the mollusc, the fish, the reptile, them mammal, man! And all so that you might sit in the gallery of a coal mine and operate the super-hyper-adding machine with the great toe of your right foot!

ZERO

Well, then—I ain't so bad, after all.

CHARLES

You're a failure, Zero, a failure. A waste product. A slave to a contraption of steel and iron. The animal's instincts, but not his strength and skill. The animal's appetites, but not his unashamed indulgence of them. True, you move and eat and digest and excrete and reproduce. But any microscopic organism can do as much. Well—time's up! Back you go—back to your sunless groove—the raw material of slums and wars—the ready prey of the first jingo or demagogue or political adventurer who takes the trouble to play upon your ignorance and credulity and provincialism. You poor, spineless, brainless boob—I'm sorry for you!

Zero

[*Falling to his knees*]: Then keep me here! Don't send me back! Let me stay!

Charles

Get up. Didn't I tell you I can't do anything for you? Come on, time's up!

Zero

I can't! I can't! I'm afraid to go through it all again.

Charles

You've got to, I tell you. Come on, now!

Zero

What did you tell me so much for? Couldn't you just let me go, thinkin' everythin' was goin' to be all right?

Charles

You wanted to know, didn't you?

Zero

How did I know what you were goin' to tell me? Now I can't stop thinkin' about it! I can't stop thinkin'! I'll be thinkin' about it all the time.

Charles

All right! I'll do the best I can for you. I'll send a girl with you to keep you company.

Zero

A girl? What for? What good will a girl do me?

Charles

She'll help make you forget.

Zero

[*Eagerly*]: She will? Where is she?

Charles

Wait a minute, I'll call her. [*He calls in a loud voice*]: Oh! Hope! Yoo-hoo! [*He turns his head aside and says in the manner of a ventriloquist imitating a distant feminine voice*]: Ye-es. [*Then in his own voice*]: Come here, will you? There's a fellow who wants you to take him back. [*Ventriloquously again*]: All right. I'll be right over, Charlie dear. [*He turns to* Zero]: Kind of familiar, isn't she? Charlie dear!

Zero

What did you say her name is?

CHARLES

Hope. H-o-p-e.

ZERO

Is she good-lookin'?

CHARLES

Is she good-looking! Oh, boy, wait until you see her! She's a blonde with big blue eyes and red lips and little white teeth and——

ZERO

Say, that listens good to me. Will she be long?

CHARLES

She'll be here right away. There she is now! Do you see her?

ZERO

No. Where?

CHARLES

Out in the corridor. No, not there. Over farther. To the right. Don't you see her blue dress? And the sunlight on her hair?

ZERO

Oh, sure! Now I see her! What's the matter with me, anyhow? Say, she's some jane! Oh, you baby vamp!

CHARLES

She'll make you forget your troubles.

ZERO

What troubles are you talkin' about?

CHARLES

Nothing.   Go on.   Don't keep her waiting.

ZERO

You bet I won't!   Oh, Hope!   Wait for me!   I'll be right with you!   I'm on my way!   [*He stumbles out eagerly.*]

[JOE *bursts into uproarious laughter.*]

CHARLES

[*Eyeing him in surprise and anger*]:   What in hell's the matter with you?

JOE

[*Shaking with laughter*]:   Did you get that?   He thinks he saw somebody and he's following her!   [*He rocks with laughter.*]

CHARLES

[*Punching him in the jaw*]:   Shut your face!

JOE

[*Nursing his jaw*]: What's the idea? Can't I even laugh when I see something funny?

CHARLES

Funny! You keep your mouth shut or I'll show you something funny. Go on, hustle out of here and get something to clean up this mess with. There's another fellow moving in. Hurry now.

[*He makes a threatening gesture. JOE exits hastily. CHARLES goes to chair and seats himself. He looks weary and dispirited.*]

CHARLES

[*Shaking his head*]: Hell, I'll tell the world this is a lousy job! [*He takes a flask from his pocket, uncorks it, and slowly drains it.*]

CURTAIN

SAMUEL FRENCH STAFF

Nate Collins
President

Ken Dingledine
Director of Operations,
Vice President

Bruce Lazarus
Executive Director,
General Counsel

Rita Maté
Director of Finance

ACCOUNTING
Lori Thimsen | Director of Licensing Compliance
Nehal Kumar | Senior Accounting Associate
Glenn Halcomb | Royalty Administration
Jessica Zheng | Accounts Receivable
Andy Lian | Accounts Payable
Charlie Sou | Accounting Associate
Joann Mannello | Orders Administrator

BUSINESS AFFAIRS
Caitlin Bartow | Assistant to the Executive Director

CORPORATE COMMUNICATIONS
Abbie Van Nostrand | Director of Corporate
Communications

CUSTOMER SERVICE AND LICENSING
Brad Lohrenz | Director of Licensing Development
Laura Lindson | Licensing Services Manager
Kim Rogers | Theatrical Specialist
Matthew Akers | Theatrical Specialist
Ashley Byrne | Theatrical Specialist
Jennifer Carter | Theatrical Specialist
Annette Storckman | Theatrical Specialist
Dyan Flores | Theatrical Specialist
Sarah Weber | Theatrical Specialist
Nicholas Dawson | Theatrical Specialist
David Kimple | Theatrical Specialist

EDITORIAL
Amy Rose Marsh | Literary Manager
Ben Coleman | Literary Associate

MARKETING
Ryan Pointer | Marketing Manager
Courtney Kochuba | Marketing Associate
Chris Kam | Marketing Associate

PUBLICATIONS AND PRODUCT DEVELOPMENT
Joe Ferreira | Product Development Manager
David Geer | Publications Manager
Charlyn Brea | Publications Associate
Tyler Mullen | Publications Associate
Derek P. Hassler | Musical Products Coordinator
Zachary Orts | Musical Materials Coordinator

OPERATIONS
Casey McLain | Operations Supervisor
Elizabeth Minski | Office Coordinator, Reception
Coryn Carson | Office Coordinator, Reception

SAMUEL FRENCH BOOKSHOP (LOS ANGELES)
Joyce Mehess | Bookstore Manager
Cory DeLair | Bookstore Buyer
Sonya Wallace | Bookstore Associate
Tim Coultas | Bookstore Associate
Alfred Contreras | Shipping & Receiving

LONDON OFFICE
Anne-Marie Ashman | Accounts Assistant
Felicity Barks | Rights & Contracts Associate
Steve Blacker | Bookshop Associate
David Bray | Customer Services Associate
Robert Cooke | Assistant Buyer
Stephanie Dawson | Amateur Licensing Associate
Simon Ellison | Retail Sales Manager
Robert Hamilton | Amateur Licensing Associate
Peter Langdon | Marketing Manager
Louise Mappley | Amateur Licensing Associate
James Nicolau | Despatch Associate
Martin Phillips | Librarian
Panos Panayi | Company Accountant
Zubayed Rahman | Despatch Associate
Steve Sanderson | Royalty Administration Supervisor
Douglas Schatz | Acting Executive Director
Roger Sheppard | I.T. Manager
Debbie Simmons | Licensing Sales Team Leader
Peter Smith | Amateur Licensing Associate
Garry Spratley | Customer Service Manager
David Webster | UK Operations Director
Sarah Wolf | Rights Director